# Enid Blyton

Summer Term at
## ST CLARE'S

HODDER CHILDREN'S BOOKS

First published in Great Britain in 1943 by Methuen & Co. Ltd
This edition published in 2016 by Hodder and Stoughton Ltd

1 3 5 7 9 10 8 6 4 2

A CIP catalogue record for this book is available from the British Library.

ISBN 978 1 444 93001 6

Printed in Great Britain by Clays Ltd, St Ives plc

The paper and board used in this book are made from
wood from responsible sources.

Hodder Children's Books
An imprint of Hachette Children's Group
Part of Hodder and Stoughton
Carmelite House
50 Victoria Embankment
London EC4Y 0DZ

An Hachette UK Company
www.hachette.co.uk

www.hachettechildrens.co.uk

# Contents

# 1

# Going back to school

'Four weeks' holiday!' said Pat O'Sullivan, as she sat up in bed the first morning of the Easter holidays. 'How lovely! Hope it's good weather!'

Her twin yawned and turned over. 'How nice not to have to get up as soon as the school bell goes,' she said, sleepily. 'I'm going to have another snooze.'

'Well, I'm not,' said Pat, hopping out of bed. 'Oh, Isabel – it's a simply perfect day! Do get up and let's go round the garden.'

But Isabel was asleep again. Pat dressed and ran downstairs. She felt happy and excited. The first day of the holidays was always grand. Everything at home looked so new and exciting and welcoming. Even the staid brown hens in the yard seemed to cluck a welcome!

School is lovely – but holidays are grand too, thought Pat. Oh, there's the first daffodil coming out – and look at those scillas – exactly the colour of the April sky!

Both the twins enjoyed the first day of the holidays in their own way. Isabel lazed around, peaceful and happy. Pat rushed here, there and everywhere, seeing everybody and everything. Their mother laughed to see the different ways in which they enjoyed themselves.

'You're as like as two peas to look at,' she said, 'but you often act in quite the opposite way. I hope this lovely weather goes on – you'll be quite nice and brown! Well – make the most of it, my dears, because your four weeks will soon go!'

'Oh, Mother – four weeks is a lovely long time – simply ages!' said Pat.

But although it seemed ages at first, it began to slip by very quickly after the first few days! The twins were astonished to find that a week had gone by – and then ten days – and then a fortnight!

'Cousin Alison is coming to spend the last two weeks with us, isn't she, Mother?' said Pat. 'When is she coming? This week?'

'On Thursday,' said Mrs O'Sullivan. 'By the way, her mother said to me on the telephone yesterday that she is much better for being a term at St Clare's – not nearly so vain and silly.'

'That's quite right,' said Isabel, thinking of the teasing and scolding her feather-headed cousin had had at St Clare's the last term. 'She learnt quite a lot of lessons – well, so did we the first term too. I'm glad you sent us there, Mother. It's a fine school. I'm already beginning to look forward to going back. Summer term ought to be grand!'

'Two more weeks,' said Pat. 'I say – won't it be fun to play tennis again? I wonder if we'll play any matches? Isabel and I were tennis captains at Redroofs, our old school. But I expect St Clare's tennis is a pretty high standard.'

'Let's mark out the court and play a few games,' said Isabel, eagerly. But Mrs O'Sullivan shook her head.

'Not in April,' she said. 'You would spoil the lawn. Ring up Katie Johnston and see if you can fix up a four on her hard court.'

It was all because of poor Isabel's eagerness to have a few practice games at tennis that the rest of the holidays were spoilt! They went over to Katie Johnston's, and played a tennis four there, with another girl, Winnie Ellis. Winnie played a very poor game, and quite spoilt it for the others.

Katie apologized for Winnie when she had the twins alone for a minute. 'Can't think what has happened to her today,' she said. 'She usually plays such a good game. She's sending everything into the net. She says her head aches, so maybe she isn't very well.'

Poor Winnie was certainly not well. She went down with mumps that evening, and her mother rang up Katie's parents at once.

'I'm so very sorry,' she said, 'but Winnie has mumps! I hope Katie has had it. Otherwise she will be in quarantine, I'm afraid.'

'Yes, Katie's had it, thank goodness,' said Mrs Johnston. 'But I don't know about the other two girls who were here playing tennis today – the O'Sullivan twins. I must ring up their mother and tell them.'

The telephone rang that evening as the twins were having supper with their parents. Mrs O'Sullivan went to answer it. She soon came back, looking a little worried.

'What's the matter?' asked Mr O'Sullivan.

'That was Mrs Johnston,' said the twins' mother. 'Pat and Isabel went over to Katie's to play tennis today – and the fourth girl was Winnie Ellis. She has just developed mumps this evening – and the twins haven't had it!'

'Well, Mother, we didn't breathe her breath or anything,' said Pat. 'We shall be all right.'

'I hope you will, dear,' said her mother. 'But the thing is – you'll both be in quarantine now – and the quarantine for mumps is rather long. You won't be able to go back to school at the beginning of the term, I'm afraid.'

The twins stared at her in dismay. 'Oh, Mother! Don't let's miss the beginning of term! It's one of the nicest parts. Can't we possibly go back in time?'

'Well, you certainly can't, of course, if you get the mumps,' said Mother. 'I'll see the doctor and find out exactly how long you will have to be away.'

Alas for the twins! The doctor said firmly that they could not go back to school for just over a week after the beginning of term. Pat and Isabel could have cried with disappointment.

'Well, well – anyone would think you liked school, the way you are looking,' said their father, laughing at their gloomy faces. 'I should have thought you would have been pleased at the chance of an extra week's holiday.'

'Not when everyone else is back at school bagging the best desks and hearing all the holiday news and seeing if there are any new girls,' said Pat. 'The first week is lovely, settling in together. Oh, blow Winnie Ellis! What did she want to go and have mumps for, and spoil things for us?'

'Well, these things do happen,' said Mother. 'Never mind. Try to enjoy your extra week. Keep out in the open air as much as you can, and let's hope you don't develop the mumps, either of you!'

During their quarantine time the twins could not go out to tea, and could have no one in to play with them, so they felt rather dull. They were glad to have each other, especially when the day came for all the girls to return to St Clare's for the summer term.

'I wonder if they'll miss us?' said Pat.

'Of course they will,' said Isabel. 'Our Cousin Alison will tell them what's happened to us. Lucky for Alison she didn't come and stay with us before we were in quarantine, or she'd have been caught like this too! Oh blow, blow, blow! What's the time? They'll all be catching the train now, and gabbling like anything in the carriages.'

'Wonder if there are any new girls?' said Pat. 'Or any new teachers? Oh dear – do you remember the tricks that Janet played on poor old Mam'zelle last term? I nearly died of laughter!'

'We shan't be able to share the tuck-boxes,' said Isabel, gloomily. 'All the cakes and things will be eaten before we get back. Oh, how I wish we were back today. Old Janet will be there – and Hilary – and Doris – and Kathleen – and Lucy and Margery – though *they* may have gone up into the second or third form, I suppose – and Sheila will be back, and Tessie.'

'Let's not think about it,' said Pat. 'Do you feel as if

you are getting the mumps, Isabel? Have you got a head-ache or a pain in the jaw or neck or anything?'

'Not a thing,' said Isabel. 'I say, wouldn't it be perfectly awful if we got mumps on the very last day of our quarantine and couldn't go back even then!'

'Anyone would think you disliked your home thoroughly!' said Mrs O'Sullivan, coming into the room. 'Well, it's nice to think you look forward to school so much. But do be sensible girls and make the most of this last week. I don't think you will get the mumps, so just be happy and look forward to going back next week.'

They tried to take their mother's advice. It was lovely weather, and they were out in the garden all day long, helping the gardener, or lazing in the hammock. But the time went very slowly, and each night the twins looked anxiously at each other to see if they had any sign of the mumps.

At last the final day of their quarantine came and in the evening the doctor arrived to make quite sure they could go back to school. He smiled cheerfully at them as he examined them, and then made their hearts sink with his next words.

'Well, my dears – I'm afraid – I'm very much afraid – that you'll have to go back to school tomorrow!'

The twins had looked full of dismay at his first words – but as he finished the sentence they beamed, and yelled with delight.

'Hurrah! We can go to school tomorrow. Hurrah! Mother, can we go and pack?'

'It's all done,' said Mrs O'Sullivan, smiling. 'I thought you were quite all right – so I packed today for you. Yes – even your tuck-boxes!'

So the next day up to London went the twins with their mother, and were put into the train for St Clare's. They were happy and excited. They would soon see all their friends again, and be lost in the excitements of school-life. They would sit in class under Mam'zelle's stern eye, they would giggle at Janet's tricks, and they would hear all the latest news. What fun!

The train sped away from the platform. It seemed to take ages to get to the station that served St Clare's. At last it drew up, and out got the two girls, shouting to the porter to get their luggage. Usually the mistresses saw to the luggage and looked after everything, tickets included – but as they were by themselves, the twins had to do all this. They quite enjoyed it.

They got a taxi, had their luggage put in, and set off to the big white building in the distance, whose tall twin towers overlooked the beautiful valley.

'Good old St Clare's,' said Pat, as she saw the building coming nearer and nearer. 'It's nice to see you again. I wonder what all the girls are doing, Isabel?'

They were at tea when the twins arrived. It was strange to arrive alone, and to have the great front door opened to them by Jane, looking very smart indeed.

'Hallo, Jane!' cried the twins. 'Where's everyone?'

'Having tea,' answered Jane. 'You'd better go along in before everything's eaten up!'

The twins ran to the big dining-hall and opened the door. A great babel of sound came to their ears – the girls all talking together happily. No one saw them at first. Then Janet happened to glance up and saw the twins standing at the door, still in their coats and hats.

'Pat! Isabel!' she yelled. 'Look, Hilary, look Kathleen, they're back! Hurrah!'

She jumped up and rushed to greet them. With a look at the astonished Miss Roberts, the mistress who was at the head of the first-form table, Kathleen and Hilary did the same. They dragged the twins to their table, and made room for them. Miss Roberts nodded at them and smiled.

'Glad you're back!' she said. 'You can take off your hats and coats and hang them over your chairs for now. I don't know if these greedy first formers have left much for you to eat, but I've no doubt we can get more from the kitchen if not!'

How good it was to be back among the girls once more! What fun to have questions hurled at them, and to call back answers! How friendly everyone was, clapping them on the back, and smiling with welcoming eyes! The twins felt very happy indeed.

'How are the mumps?'

'So you've turned up at last!'

'Your Cousin Alison told us the news. Bad luck you couldn't come back the first day!'

'Mam'zelle has missed you terribly – haven't you, Mam'zelle?'

'Ah, *ma chère* Pat, the French class is no longer the

same without you and Isabel. There is now no one to shout at and say, "*C'est abominable*!"' said Mam'zelle, in her deep voice.

'It's good to be back!' said Isabel, helping herself to bread and butter and jam. 'I say – we've got our tuck-boxes with us. We must open them tomorrow.'

'We've finished all that was in ours,' said Hilary. 'Never mind – two or three of us have birthdays this term and you can have a double share of birthday cake to make up for missing our tuck-boxes!'

Only four or five girls around the big table said nothing. They were all new girls, and they did not know the twins. They stared at them in silence, thinking that the two must be very popular to get such a welcome. Pat and Isabel took a quick look at the strange girls, but had no time to size them up for they were so busy exchanging news and eating.

Plenty of time to know the new girls afterwards, thought Pat. My, it's good to be back at St Clare's again!

# 2

# Settling down again

It really was lovely to be back at school again, and to hear the familiar chattering and laughing, to see the piles of books everywhere, and to hear the familiar groans of 'Who's taken my pen?' or 'Gracious, I'll never get all this prep done!'

It was good to see the smiling mistresses, and to catch a glimpse of Winifred James, the dignified head girl. It was fun to have a word with Belinda Towers, the sports captain. The twins greeted her with beaming smiles, for they liked her immensely. She was one of the top formers, but because she arranged all the matches for the whole school, she was much better known to the lower forms than the other big girls.

'Hallo, twins!' she said, stopping to greet them after tea. 'What about tennis this term? I hope you're good. We want to play St Christopher's and Oakdene, and beat them hollow. Have you played any in the hols?'

'Only once,' said Pat. 'We used to be good at our old school, but I don't expect we shall shine much at St Clare's.'

'My word, haven't you changed since you first came two terms ago!' said Janet, with a sly smile. 'The stuck-up twins would at once have said that they were champions at tennis!'

'Shut up, Janet,' said Pat, uncomfortably. She never liked being reminded of the way she and Isabel had behaved the first term they had arrived at St Clare's. They had been called the stuck-up twins then, and had had a very difficult time.

'Don't mind Janet's teasing,' said Lucy Oriell, slipping her arm through Pat's. 'You know her bark is worse than her bite. Pat, I shan't see as much of you this term as I'd like, because I've been moved up into the second form.'

'I thought you would be,' said Pat, sadly. She and Isabel were very fond of Lucy. Lucy's father had had an accident the term before, which meant he could no longer do his usual work, and for a while everyone had thought that the popular, merry-eyed Lucy would have to leave. But there was a chance that she could win a scholarship and stay on at St Clare's, for she was very clever and quick. So she had been moved up and would now work with the scholarship girls.

'Margery's been moved up too,' said Lucy. Margery came up at that moment, a tall, older-looking girl. She gave the twins a slap on the back.

'Hallo!' she said. 'Did Lucy tell you the sad news? I'm in the second form too, and I feel very superior indeed to you tiddlers! And gosh – I'm working hard! Aren't I, Lucy?'

'You are,' said Lucy. Margery was her friend, and the two had been glad to be moved up together.

'Who else has been moved up?' asked Isabel, as they all went to the common-room together.

'Vera Johns, but that's all,' said Janet. 'Otherwise our form is the same – except for the new girls, of course. By the way, your Cousin Alison has palled up with one of them – an American girl, stiff-rich, called Sadie Greene. There she is, over there.'

The twins looked for Sadie. There was no mistaking her. Although she wore the school uniform it was plain that her mother had got the very best material possible and had had it made by the very best dressmaker! It was plain too that her hair was permed, and her nails were polished so highly that each small finger-tip shone like a little mirror.

'Golly!' said Pat, staring. 'What a fashion victim. What's she been sent to St Clare's for?'

'Can't imagine,' said Janet. 'She thinks of nothing but her appearance, and nearly drives poor Mam'zelle mad. She has the most atrocious French accent you ever heard, and her American drawl is worst Hollywood. You should hear her say "Twenty-four!" The best she can manage is "Twenny-fourr-r-r-r-r!" no matter how many times Miss Roberts makes her repeat it. Honestly we've had some fun in English classes, I can tell you. Sadie's not a bad sort though – awfully good tempered and generous really. But she's jolly bad for that silly cousin of yours. They walk together whenever we go out and talk of nothing but clothes and haircuts and film stars!'

'We'll have to take Alison in hand,' said Pat, firmly.

'I thought she looked a bit more feather-brained than usual when I saw her just now. I say – who's that? What a wild-looking creature!'

'That's our Carlotta,' said Hilary with a grin. 'She's half-Spanish, and has a fiercer temper than Mam'zelle's, and that's saying something! She speaks very badly, and has the most awful ideas – but she's pretty good fun. I can see a first-class row boiling up between her and Mam'zelle some day!'

'Oh, it *is* good to be back,' said Pat, thoroughly enjoying hearing all this exciting news. 'The new girls sound thrilling. I did hope there would be some. But I'm sorry the other three have gone up into the second form – I shall miss Lucy and Margery especially.'

Pat and Isabel had no prep to do that night but they had to unpack and put away their things instead. They left the noisy common-room and went upstairs to their dormitory.

Hilary called after them. 'You're in Number Six, twins. I'm there, and Janet, and Prudence Arnold, a new girl, and Carlotta Brown. And Kathleen and Sheila are there too. You'll see which are your cubicles.'

The twins went up the broad stairway and made their way to the big dormitory. It was divided into eight cubicles, which had white curtains hung round them that could be pulled back or drawn round, just as the girls wished. Pat found their cubicles at once. They were side by side.

'Come on, let's be quick,' said Pat. 'I want to get down and have a talk again. There are still three new girls to hear about. I rather liked one of them – the one with the turned-up nose and crinkly eyes.'

'Yes, I liked her too,' said Isabel. 'She looked a monkey. I noticed she and Janet ragged each other a lot. I bet she's good at tricks too. I say – it looks as if we'll have some fun this term, Pat!'

They unpacked happily, and stowed their things away in the drawers of their chests. They hung up their dresses and coats in the cupboard, and set out the few things they had for their dressing-table. They put out the pictures of their father and mother, and their brushes and mirrors.

'I expect we'd better go and see Matron and Miss Theobald,' said Pat, when they had finished. So down they went and made their way to Matron's room. She was there, sorting out piles of laundry. 'Come in!' she called in her cheerful voice. She looked up and beamed at the twins.

'Two bad eggs back again!' she said. 'Dear, dear – and I've had such a peaceful time without you for a whole week of term. Why couldn't you get the mumps and give me a little longer spell? Well – all I say is – don't you dare to go down with the mumps now, and start an epidemic of it!'

The twins grinned. Everyone liked Matron. She was full of common sense and fun – but woe betide anyone who lost too many hankies, tore their sheets, or didn't darn their stockings at once! Matron descended on them immediately, and many a time the twins had had to go to Matron's room and try in vain to explain away missing articles.

'We're glad to be back,' said Pat. 'We're looking forward to tennis and swimming, Matron.'

'Well, remember that your swimming-costumes have to be brought to me after swimming,' said Matron. 'No screwing them up and stuffing away into drawers with dry things! Now run away, both of you – unless you want a dose out of a nice new bottle of medicine!'

The twins laughed. Matron had the largest bottles of medicine they had ever seen anywhere. There was a big new one on the mantelpiece. Matron picked it up and shook it. 'Try it!' she said.

But the twins fled. Downstairs they went to see Miss Theobald, the wise and kindly head mistress. They knocked at the sitting-room door.

'Come in!' said a voice, and in they went. Miss Theobald was sitting at her desk, writing. She took off her glasses and smiled at the blushing twins. They liked the head mistress very much, but they always felt nervous in front of her.

'Well, twins?' she said. 'I still don't know which is which! Are *you* Patricia?' She looked at Isabel as she said this and Isabel shook her head.

'No, I'm Isabel,' she said, with a laugh. 'I've got a few more freckles on my nose than Pat has. That's about the only way to tell us at present.'

Miss Theobald laughed. 'Well, that's an easy way to tell one from the other when you are both in front of

15

me,' she said, 'but it wouldn't be very helpful when there was only one of you. Now listen, twins – I want you to work hard this term, because Miss Roberts thinks you should go up into the second form next term. So just see what you can do! I should like you to try for top places this term. You both have good brains and should be able to do it.'

The twins felt proud. Of course they would try! What fun it would be to go up into the next form – and how pleased their parents would be.

They went out of the room determined to work hard – and to play tennis hard and swim well. 'Thank goodness we didn't get the mumps,' said Pat, happily, as they went back to the common-room. 'Wouldn't it have been awful to have missed more weeks of the summer term?'

It was supper-time when they reached the common-room and the girls were pouring out to go to the dining-hall, chattering loudly. Janet was arm-in-arm with the new girl, the one with the turned-up nose and crinkly eyes.

'Hallo, Pat, hallo, Isabel,' she said. 'Come and be introduced to the Bad Girl of the Form – Bobby Ellis!'

Bobby grinned, and her eyes became more crinkled than ever. She certainly looked naughty – and there was a sort of don't-care air about her that the twins liked at once.

'Is your name really Bobby?' asked Pat. 'It's a boy's name.'

'I know,' said Bobby. 'But my name is Roberta and the short name for Robert is Bobby, you know – so I'm always called Bobby too. I've heard a lot about you two twins.'

'Good things I hope, not bad,' said Isabel, laughing.

'Wouldn't you like to know!' said Bobby, with a twinkle, and went off with Janet.

It was fun to sit down at supper-time again and hear the familiar chatter going on, fun to take big thick slices of bread and spread it with potted meat or jam. Fun to drink the milky cocoa and yell for the sugar. Everything was so friendly and jolly, and the twins loved it all. Afterwards the girls returned to the common-room and put on the radio or the record player. Some of the girls did their knitting, some read, and some merely lazed.

By the time that bedtime came the twins felt as if they had been back at school for weeks! It seemed quite impossible to think they had only been there a few hours.

They went upstairs yawning. 'What's the work like this term?' asked Pat, poking her head into Janet's cubicle as they undressed.

'Fierce,' said Janet. 'It always is in the summer term, don't you think so? I suppose it seems extra difficult because we all so badly want to be out in the sunshine – but honestly Miss Roberts is driving us like slaves this term. Some of us will have to go up into the second form next term, and I suppose she doesn't want us to be backward in anything. My goodness, the maths we've had the last week! You just wait and see.'

But not even the thought of Miss Roberts being fierce

with maths could make the twins feel unhappy that first night! They cuddled down into their narrow beds and fell asleep at once, looking forward to the next day with enjoyment.

# 3

# Back in Miss Roberts's class

The twins awoke before the bell went the next morning. They lay whispering to each other whilst the May sunshine shone warmly in at the window. Then the bell went and the eight girls got out of bed, some with a leap, like Carlotta and the twins, some with a groan like Sheila, who always hated turning out of her warm bed, winter or summer.

They met their Cousin Alison coming out of her dormitory arm-in-arm with the American girl, Sadie Greene. They stared at Alison, because she had done her hair in quite a different way.

'Alison! What have you done to your hair?' said Pat. 'It looks awful. Do you think you are a film star or something?'

'Sadie says I look grand like this,' said Alison, setting her little mouth in an obstinate line. 'Sadie says . . .'

'That's all Alison can say nowadays,' remarked Janet. 'She's like a record always set to say, "Sadie says . . . Sadie says . . . Sadie says . . ." '

Everyone laughed. 'It's sure a wunnerful way of fixing the hair,' said Doris, with a very good imitation of Sadie's American accent. Sadie laughed. She was very good tempered.

'I don't know what Miss Roberts will say though,' went on Doris. 'She isn't very keen on fancy hair styles, Alison.'

'Well, but Sadie says . . .' began Alison, in an injured sort of voice – and at once all the girls took up the refrain.

'Sadie says . . . Sadie says . . . Sadie says!' they chanted in a sort of chorus, whilst Doris jumped up on to a nearby chair and beat time for the chanting. Alison's eyes filled with the easy tears she always knew how to shed.

'You can see your cousin can turn on the water tap just as easily as last term,' said Janet, in her clear voice. Alison turned away to hide her face. She knew that the girls had no patience with her tears. Sadie slipped her arm through hers.

'Aw, come on, sugar-baby,' she said. 'You're a cute little thing, and I won't let them tease you!'

'I can't think how your cousin can make friends with that vulgar American girl,' said a soft voice at Pat's side. 'It's good thing you've come. Sadie has a very bad influence on the class.'

Pat turned and saw the girl called Prudence Arnold. She didn't know whether she liked the look of her or not. Prudence was pretty, but her mouth was hard, and her eyes, set too close together, were a pale blue.

The breakfast bell went and saved Pat the bother of answering. She ran down the stairs with the others and whispered to Janet. 'Is that Prudence? She looks awfully goody-goody.'

'Yes, you'd better mind your Ps and Qs with her!' said Janet. 'She's so good she'll burst with it one day –

and as for playing a trick on anyone, well the thought of it would send her into a fit. You should have seen her face one day last week when I flipped a rubber at Hilary in class. It was enough to turn the milk sour. Oh and by the way – according to her she's related to half the lords and ladies in the kingdom. Get her on to the subject – she's funny!'

'No talking now please,' said Miss Roberts as the girls stood for grace to be said. Pat took a quick look at Prudence. The girl was standing with her head bent and her eyes shut, the very picture of goodness.

Now Lucy Oriell is *really* good, thought Pat, glancing at Lucy, and I like her awfully, and did from the first – and yet I don't take to Prudence at all, and *she* sounds good too. Perhaps it is because she hasn't any sense of fun, and Lucy has. I wonder if she's as clever as Lucy at lessons. Well, we shall soon see.

That morning Miss Roberts read out the class marks for the week, and the last new girl, Pamela Boardman, was top with ninety-three marks out of a hundred. Prudence Arnold was only halfway down the list. Sadie, Alison, Carlotta and Doris vied for places at the bottom.

'Pamela, you have done very well for the first week,' said Miss Roberts. 'I can see you set yourself a high standard, and you work steadily in each subject. Considering that you are the youngest in the form – not yet fourteen – this is very good.'

All the girls stared at Pamela, who was sitting upright at her desk, red with pleasure. The twins looked at her

21

curiously. They were nearly fifteen, and it seemed marvellous to them that a thirteen-year-old should be top of their form.

'She's very small even for thirteen,' thought Pat. 'And she's pale now that she's not red any more. She looks as if she worked too hard!'

Pamela was not very attractive looking. She wore big glasses, and her straight hair was tightly plaited down her back. She had a very earnest face, and paid the greatest attention to everything Miss Roberts said.

Miss Roberts had some more to say. She flipped at the marks list with her first finger and then looked firmly at Alison, Sadie, Doris and Carlotta.

'You are all bottom,' she said. 'Well, we know *someone* has to be bottom – but nobody needs to be quite so very low down as all of you are. Sit up, Sadie! Carlotta, there is no need to grin round the class like that. It isn't funny to get so few marks in any and every subject!'

Carlotta stopped grinning round and scowled. Not even her school uniform could make her look ordinary. She glared at Miss Roberts.

Miss Roberts took no notice of the scowl or the glare, but went calmly on. 'Doris, you have been in my form for four terms now, and I'm really tired of seeing you at the bottom still. You will have extra coaching this term, because you really mustn't stay in my form much longer.'

'Yes, Miss Roberts,' murmured poor Doris. The girls glanced at her, trying to cheer her up. Doris was a real dunce and knew it – and yet of all the girls in the school she could be the very funniest, sending the class into squeals of laughter by her imitations of mistresses and other girls. Everyone liked her, even the mistresses who laboured so hard trying to teach her.

'Now you, Alison,' began Miss Roberts again, looking at the twins' cousin with the intention of telling her that she also could do better, 'now you, Alison . . .' Then she stopped and looked at the girl carefully.

'Alison,' she said, 'there is something very strange about you this morning. It seems to me that you have forgotten to do your hair.'

'Oh no, Miss Roberts,' began Alison, eagerly. 'Sadie showed me a new way. She said I had the kind of face that . . .'

'Alison, you don't really mean to tell me that your hair is done like that on *pur*pose!' said Miss Roberts, in pretended horror. Alison subsided at once, and the girls giggled. Alison really did look a little silly with her hair done in a fancy way. Miss Roberts never could stand what she called 'frippery' in dress or hair style.

'Much as I hate you to lose any part of my lesson, Alison,' she said, 'I must ask you to go and do something to your hair that will make you look a little less amazing.'

'I thought she'd be sent out to do her hair properly.' whispered Janet to Pat. Miss Roberts's sharp ears caught the whisper.

'No talking,' she said. 'We'll now get on with the lesson. Open your maths books at page sixteen. Pat and Isabel, bring your books up to my desk, please, and I will try and explain to you what the class did last week when you were away. The rest of you get on with what you began yesterday.'

In a little while all was silence as the class applied itself to its work. Alison slipped back into the room quietly, her cheeks flaming. Her hair was now taken down and brushed back properly, and she looked what she was, a fourteen-year-old schoolgirl. Sadie sent her a look of sympathy.

Prudence and Pamela bent their heads almost to their desks, so concentrated were they on their task. They sat next to each other. Prudence took a quick look at Pamela's book to see if her own sums showed the same answers. Janet nudged Hilary.

'Our pious little Prudence isn't above having a peep at Pam's work!' she whispered, opening her desk to hide the fact that she was speaking. Hilary nodded. She was about to open her own desk and make a remark, but Miss Roberts's eye caught hers and she decided not to. Miss Roberts didn't seem to be standing any nonsense that term! She meant her class to do well, and to make a good showing when most of it went up into Miss Jenks's form the next term!

Pat and Isabel stood beside Miss Roberts struggling to understand what she was explaining. Their five weeks' holiday had made them rusty, and it was difficult to get back the habit of concentration again. But at last they understood and went back to their places to work.

Miss Roberts got up to go round the class.

A suppressed giggle made her look round. Bobby Ellis had balanced a sheet of blotting-paper on the bent head of the unsuspecting Prudence. It sat there, moving slightly whenever Prudence turned her head a little to refer to her textbook. Then it floated gently to the ground, much to Prudence's surprise.

'I imagine that, as you find time to play about with blotting-paper, Roberta, you have also found time to do every one of the sums set,' said Miss Roberts in a cold sort of voice. Bobby said nothing. She hadn't done even half the sums.

'Well, if you haven't done all the sums, and got them right too, by the time I get round to you, you will stay in at break and do them then,' said Miss Roberts. 'Prudence, pick up the blotting-paper and put it on my desk.'

'Miss Roberts, I didn't know anything about what Bobby was doing,' said Prudence, anxiously. 'I was quite lost in my work. I . . .'

'Quite so, Prudence,' said Miss Roberts. 'Now pick up the blotting-paper please and get lost again.'

Poor Bobby lost her time at break. There was no doubt about it – Miss Roberts was on the war-path that term!

'What did I tell you?' said Janet, when the morning ended at last, and the girls trooped out to wash for lunch. 'What a morning! Alison sent out to do her hair again – most of us scolded – Bobby kept in for break – Janet ticked off for talking twice – Doris pulled up for dreaming in geography – Carlotta sent out of the room for answering back – and double the amount of prep we usually have! Golly, this *is* going to be a term!'

# 4

# The five new girls

In a day or two the twins had settled down so well again that no one even remembered they had been late in coming back. They felt that it was a little unfair that the teachers so soon forgot this, for once or twice they were scolded for not knowing things that the rest of the class had been taught during the first week.

But the twins had good brains and soon caught up with the others. They had always loved the summer term at their old school, and they found that it was just as nice at St Clare's. There was no lacrosse that term, of course, but instead there were tennis and swimming – and they were grand!

There were eight courts at St Clare's, and Belinda Towers, who had charge of them, drew up a careful timetable so that every girl could have her turn at tennis practice. Miss Wilton, the sports mistress, was an excellent coach, and soon picked out the girls who would do well.

Margery Fenworthy, one of the old first formers who had gone up into the second form, was brilliant at tennis, as she was at all sports. Miss Wilton was delighted with her.

'She's so strong,' she told Belinda, 'and she has a lovely

style. Watch her serve, Belinda. See how she throws the ball up high, and gives it just the right smack when it comes down – and skims it over the top of the net. You know, I shouldn't be surprised if she wins the school championship this term, and beats all you top formers!'

'I don't mind if she does,' said Belinda, 'so long as she wins the matches against the other schools we play! Oakdene and St Christopher's are both running singles championships, you know, this term. Perhaps we can put Margery in for our player. She's better than I am.'

'Well, there's not much to choose between you,' said the sports mistress, 'except that Margery is immensely strong.'

The twins were quite good at tennis, and Miss Wilton was pleased with their style. 'Practise well and you may be in the tennis team for the first form,' she said. 'We shall be playing plenty of matches this term, so you'll have some fun if you get into the team.'

The twins flushed with pleasure, and made up their minds to practise every minute they could. They loved their school and were very anxious to do everything they could to bring it fame among other schools.

But Miss Wilton was not so pleased with their cousin Alison. Alison did not like games. 'They make me get hot and messy,' she always complained. 'I hate running about, especially in the hot weather. My hair gets all wet at the back of my neck.'

'Alison, you make me feel sick,' said Bobby Ellis, who always said straight out what she was thinking. She was a bit like Janet that way, without Janet's hot temper. 'You're nothing but a little peacock, always hoping someone's going to admire you!'

'Alison got much better last term,' said Pat, trying to stick up for her cousin. 'She really did try to get on with lacrosse.'

'Well, Sadie says . . .' began Alison, quite forgetting what the girls thought about this refrain of hers. At once the girls nearby took up the chorus.

'Sadie says . . . Sadie says . . . Sadie says . . . What does Sadie say?' they chanted.

Alison turned away in a temper. She was usually quite a good-tempered girl, but she hated being teased, and she certainly was getting a lot of it that term. She flew off to find her precious Sadie. Sadie didn't care about games either. It was difficult to find out what she did care about, with the exception of clothes, hair, nails, complexion – and the cinema!

Sadie frankly didn't try at tennis or swimming. She hated the water. So did Alison. Alison couldn't bear going in. 'It's so icy cold!' she complained, as she stood at the top of the steps leading down into the deliciously green water. She would stand there, shivering, until one of the girls gave her an exasperated push and sent her in with a gasp and a flop. Then she would come up, spluttering in fury, and glare round for the girl who had pushed her in. But Bobby or Janet or whoever it was would be well away at the top of the swimming-pool!

Only one of the new girls really took to tennis and

swimming. That was Bobby Ellis. She was a good sport, and so daring that she even pushed Miss Wilton unexpectedly into the pool, a thing that no other girl would have dared to do. Nobody ever knew what Don't-Care-Bobby would do next. She really seemed to care for nothing and nobody, and went her own sweet way regardless of rules or punishments. She was good at tennis and a fast swimmer – but not one of the other new girls was any good at sports.

Prudence was no sport. She thought games were a waste of time, but only because she was no good at them. She fancied herself clever at conversation, and was always trying to get the other girls to argue about politics.

'Oh, shut up!' Janet would say. 'Keep that sort of thing for the debating hour, for goodness' sake! If you took a bit more interest in the jolly things of life, and *did* something instead of always talking and prating and airing your wonderful opinions, you'd get on better. I consider you're a silly little empty-head, for all your talk. Golly, you can't even play a simple game of cards!'

'My father says cards lead to gambling,' said Prudence. Her father was a clergyman, and the girl had been brought up very strictly. 'My aunt, who married Sir Humphrey Bartlett . . .'

There was a groan at this. The girls were getting heartily sick of Prudence's grand relations, who were brought into the conversation whenever possible.

'Let me see,' said Bobby, pretending to be interested, 'was that the aunt who always had blue silk sheets on the beds? Or was it the one who threw a fit because the home help dared to give her a hot-water bottle with a cover that didn't match the eiderdown? Or was it the one who kept table napkins embroidered with every letter in the alphabet so that no matter what the names of her guests were, there was always a napkin with the right initial?'

Prudence flushed. She had once boasted about an aunt who had blue silk sheets for her beds, but she hadn't said anything about hot-water bottles or table napkins. Those were clever make-ups on Bobby's part. She said nothing.

'Well, go on, tell us!' said Bobby. 'We're all eager to hear the latest Society News!'

But Prudence had sense enough not to be drawn into an argument with Bobby. Clever as she was at debating things, she was no match for the quick-witted Bobby, who got all the laughs whenever she argued with any one.

Pamela Boardman was very earnest over her tennis and swimming, but she was no good at them at all. 'You see, I always had a governess before I came here,' she explained to the girls, 'and my governess didn't play games. Anyway, I was never interested in them. I loved working at lessons.'

'All work and no play makes Jack a dull boy,' said Pat. 'You're much too clever for thirteen! I think it would do you good to be bottom of the form for once, and really enjoy yourself out in the open air! You're always stewing over a book.'

Carlotta had never played tennis before, and she was quite wild at it. Miss Wilton said that she really thought Carlotta imagined the tennis net to be about two miles high, the way she hit the ball into the air, sky-high!

'Carlotta, when I was small, I played a game with my brothers called "Chimney-pot tennis",' she said solemnly to the fiery little girl. 'We sent the ball up to the roof and tried to get it down a chimney. Well, it seems to me you would be very good indeed at that game! But as you are not playing with chimney-pots, I really would be very glad if you could have a look at the net over there, and see if you can get the ball anywhere near it when you serve. Now – throw it into the air – and hit it straight towards the net!'

There would be a shriek of laughter from the watching girls as Carlotta hit wildly at the ball and, as likely as not, sent it over the wall into the kitchen-garden!

Her swimming was much the same, though she liked the water and was quite at home in it. But, as Belinda complained, she swam just like a dog, splashing out with legs and arms just anyhow.

'You swim like my dog Binks,' said Kathleen. 'He sort of scrabbles along in the water, and so do you, Carlotta!'

Sadie couldn't swim at all, and though she didn't mind the cold, as Alison did, she hated having to put her carefully done hair under a tight swimming-hat, and complained that the water ruined her complexion. So, with the exception of Bobby Ellis, the first formers voted the new girls a complete failure at sports.

'It's a pity our form have lost Margery Fenworthy,' said Isabel, as she watched the straight-limbed girl swimming the whole length of the pool under water. 'She would win the championship for the school, and wouldn't we first formers be proud!'

May was a glorious month that year, warm and sunny. Swimming was in full swing, and daily tennis made the grass become worn at the service lines. A good many of the girls had school gardens, and these patches were soon full of growing seedlings of all kinds. Gardening was the one outdoor thing that Pamela really seemed to like. She took a big patch and sowed many packets of seeds there. She bought little plants too, double-daisies, velvet pansies and pretty polyanthus to make the borders of her patch bright.

There were nature-walks over the hills and through the woods. Sadie and Carlotta knew nothing about nature, it seemed, and made some curious mistakes. When Pat exclaimed at the amount of frogs in the pond, Sadie looked at them with interest.

'I got some early frog-spawn in the spring,' said Pat, 'and I got heaps of tadpoles from it. Most of them have turned into tiny little frogs now. They're sweet.'

'Do tadpoles turn into frogs, then?' said Sadie in the greatest surprise. The girls laughed at her. They couldn't imagine how it was that Sadie knew so little about the most ordinary things.

'Didn't you ever go to school before?' said Pat.

'Well, I lived mostly in hotels in America with my mother,' said Sadie. 'I had a sort of governess but she didn't know much! You see, most of the time my mother was fighting a law case.'

'What's that?' asked Isabel.

'Well, when my father died he left a funny sort of will,' said Sadie. 'And it seemed as if all his money would go to his sisters. So Mother had to go to law about it, and it took years to settle. She won in the end – and I'm to have the money when I'm twenty-one. It's a proper fortune.'

'So you're an heiress?' said Prudence, admiringly. 'No wonder you have such nice clothes and things.'

It was the first time that Prudence had heard of Sadie's fortune. After that everyone noticed that the girl hung around Sadie continually.

'See dear Prudence sucking up to the rich heiress?' said Janet, scornfully. 'She's made friends with Pamela so that she can pick her brains – and now she's making friends with Sadie because one day she'll be rich. Nasty little humbug!'

'That's a bit unkind,' said Pat. 'After all, Sadie's kind and generous, and we all like to be friends with her because of those things, not because she's well off. And Pam's a nice little thing, though she's such a swot. I'm not friends with her because I want to pick her brains but because there's something rather nice about her, in spite of her head always being inside a book.'

'Well, stick up for Prudence if you like,' said Janet. 'I think she's a humbug. I can't stick her goody-goody ways. Can you, Bobby?'

Bobby agreed. There was no humbug about Bobby. You always knew where you were with her. She was warm, friendly and sincere for all her don't-care attitude to everyone and everything.

'We're a mixed bunch this term,' said Pat to Isabel, as she gazed round her form one morning. 'A very mixed bunch. There'll be a few bust-ups before we all shake down together!'

# 5

# Bobby plays a trick

After two or three weeks the first form began to work quite well. The girls saw that Miss Roberts meant to have her way about the work, and they soon found that it was quicker to prepare work thoroughly, than to have it all to do again after the lesson because it was carelessly prepared beforehand.

Janet badly wanted to go up with the others the next term, so she worked hard. But Bobby Ellis, who had become her firm friend, could not work hard for more than a few days at a time. After that she became bored, and then the class had some fun. For when Bobby was bored with work, she found relief in tricks and jokes. Janet had always been marvellous at these, but Bobby was ten times more ingenious!

Bobby always found the maths lesson far too long. She hated maths and could never see the use of them. 'I wish I could make the lessons ten minutes shorter,' she sighed, as she dressed one morning. 'Miss Roberts said she was going to give us an oral test at the end of maths today, and I know I shall be bottom. I can't even think what seven times eight are!'

'Well, can't you think of some way of making the

lesson short?' said Janet. 'I don't like oral maths tests any more than you do. If only we could put the clock on when Miss Roberts isn't looking!'

'She's got eyes at the back of her head,' said Bobby. 'No good doing it when she's there. If only she'd go out of the room for a minute. But she never does.'

'Can't you make her?' said Pat. 'You're always full of ideas. Go on – I dare you to make her!'

Bobby always took on any 'dare'. She looked at Pat, and grinned. 'Right!' she said. 'I'll bet you a stick of toffee to a peppermint drop that Miss Roberts disappears from our classroom during the maths lesson.'

All the girls began to feel excited. Bobby was such fun. They knew she would do something unusual!

She did. She sat lost in thought at breakfast-time, and forgot to have any marmalade with her toast. Between breakfast and the first class, which was geography, Bobby disappeared.

She went to the common-room, which was empty, for the girls were now tidying their cubicles and making their beds. She got down her writing-pad and pen, and in neat, mature writing, penned two lines.

'Kindly attend at the mistresses' common-room in the lesson after break.'

She added a squiggle at the bottom that looked like anybody's initials, popped the note into an envelope and printed Miss Roberts's name on it. Then she placed the note inside her writing-pad in readiness for when she meant to use it.

'Thought of a plan yet?' asked Janet, when Bobby rejoined the girls upstairs. 'I've made your bed for you. What have you been doing?'

'Wait and see,' said Bobby, with a grin.

Maths was the first lesson after break. The girls waited impatiently for it, wondering what was going to happen. At break they begged Bobby to tell them what she was going to do, but she wouldn't.

She slipped off to the common-room whilst the others were out in the garden. She took the note she had written, and went into Miss Jenks's classroom, next to Miss Roberts. She laid the note on Miss Jenks's desk, and then, making sure that no one had seen her, she slipped out again and went into the garden.

'Miss Jenks will see the note and think it has been left in the wrong classroom by mistake.' Bobby grinned to herself. 'She'll send one of her girls in with it to Miss Roberts – and then maybe we'll see our Miss Roberts trotting off to the mistresses' common-room. And if I don't move the hands of the clock on whilst she's gone, my name isn't Roberta Henrietta Ellis!'

All the girls trooped back when the school bell rang. They went to their classroom and waited for the mistresses to come and take the next lesson. Hilary stood at the door watching for Miss Roberts.

'Sssst! Here she is!' warned Hilary. The girls stood up at once, and became silent. Miss Roberts came in and went to her desk.

'Sit,' she said, and the girls sat down with clatters

and scrapes of their chairs.

'Now today,' said Miss Roberts, briskly, 'we will try to do a *little* better than yesterday, when Pamela was the only one who got even *one* sum right. At the end of the lesson there will be a ten minutes' oral test – and I warn you, no one is to get less than half-marks, or there will be trouble. Alison, please sit up. I don't like to see you draped over your desk like that. You are here to do maths not to act like the Sleeping Beauty and go to sleep for a hundred years!'

'Oh, Miss Roberts, *must* we have an oral test on a hot day like this?' said Alison, whose brains worked slowly in the hot weather. 'This hot sun does make me feel so sleepy at the end of the morning.'

'Well, I shall wake you up thoroughly if you seem sleepy in your oral test,' said Miss Roberts, grimly. 'Now – page twenty-seven, please. Bobby, why do you keep looking at the door?'

Bobby had had no idea that her eyes were continually on the door, waiting for it to open and a second former to appear. She jumped.

'Er – was I looking at the door?' she said, at a loss what to say, for once.

'You were,' said Miss Roberts. 'Now for a change, look at your book. Begin work, everyone!'

Bobby looked at page twenty-seven, but she didn't see the sums there. She was wondering if Miss Jenks had seen the note. What a pity if she hadn't! The whole joke would be spoilt.

But Miss Jenks had. She had not noticed it at first,

because she had put her books down on it. Then she had written something on the blackboard for the class to do, and had gone round the form to make sure they all understood what she had written. It was not until she sent Tessie to her desk to fetch a book that the note was discovered.

Tessie lifted up the books – and the note was there underneath. Tessie glanced at it and saw that Miss Roberts's name was printed on it.

'There's a note here on your desk for Miss Roberts, Miss Jenks,' she said. 'Do you suppose it was left here by mistake?'

'Bring it to me,' said Miss Jenks. Tessie took it to her. 'Yes – someone thought this was the first form, I suppose,' said Miss Jenks. 'Take it straight in to Miss Roberts, Tessie – and come straight back.'

Tessie took the note and left the room. She knocked at the door of Miss Roberts's classroom. All was complete silence inside.

Bobby's heart jumped when she heard the knock. She looked up eagerly. 'Come in!' said Miss Roberts, impatiently. She always hated interruptions to her classwork. Tessie opened the door and came in.

'Excuse me, Miss Roberts,' she said, politely, 'but Miss Jenks told me to come and give you this.'

This was better than Bobby had hoped! Now it sounded as if Miss Jenks herself had sent the note. Miss Roberts wouldn't suspect a thing. Miss Roberts took the note, nodded to Tessie, and opened the envelope.

40

She read what was inside and frowned. It was a nuisance to have to leave her class in the middle of a difficult maths lesson. Well, she would slip along straight-away whilst the form was hard at work, and see why she was wanted.

She put the note back on her desk and stood up. 'Go on with your work, please,' she said. 'I shall be away a minute or two. No talking, of course. Finish what you are doing, and work hard.'

All the girls looked up, astonished, for they guessed that Bobby somehow had been the cause of Miss Roberts's disappearance – but how could she have made Miss Jenks send in a note to get her away? They gaped round at Bobby, who grinned back in delight.

'How did you do it, Bobby?' said Janet in a whisper, as soon as the door was shut.

'Bobby! You didn't write that note, did you?' said Pat, amazed. Bobby nodded and leapt to her feet. She ran quietly to the mantelpiece and opened the glass covering of the big schoolroom clock. In a moment she had put the hands on more than ten minutes. She shut the glass with a click and returned to her place.

'You really are a monkey!' said Hilary, thrilled. Even Pamela was amused. Only Prudence looked disapproving.

'It seems rather a deceitful thing to do,' she murmured. Sadie gave her a push.

'Aw, don't be a ninny!' she said, in her American drawl. 'Can't you ever see a joke?'

'I wonder what poor Miss Roberts is doing,' said Janet.

'What did you say in the note, Bobby? How clever of you to leave it in the wrong classroom so that Tessie had to bring it in!'

'Miss Roberts is probably waiting all alone in the mistresses' common-room,' said Bobby, with her wide grin. 'I don't know how long she'll wait!'

Miss Roberts was feeling very puzzled. She had hurried to the common-room belonging to the Junior mistresses, and had found no one there. Thinking the others would come in a minute or two, she went to the window and waited. But still nobody came.

Miss Roberts tapped her foot impatiently on the floor. She hated leaving her class at any time. There were too many mischief-makers in it that term! They couldn't safely be left for two minutes. What they would be up to now she couldn't think.

'I'll go and see if Miss Jenks knows what it's all about,' she thought. So she went to the second form, and was soon questioning a surprised Miss Jenks about the supposed meeting.

'I don't know anything about it,' said Miss Jenks. 'I just sent the note in by Tessie because it was left on my desk for you by mistake. How funny, Miss Roberts!'

Miss Roberts, very much puzzled, went back to her class. She took a quick look round, but every head was bent and it seemed as if every girl was hard at work.

Too good to be true! thought Miss Roberts disbelievingly. Half the little monkeys have been playing about, and the other half talking. It's impossible to realize that when they are top formers they will all be thoroughly trustworthy, more dignified than the mistresses even, and so responsible that we could probably trust the whole running of the school to them. Who would have thought that Winifred James, our worthy head girl, was sent out of my class three times in one morning for playing up with her best friend?

Miss Roberts was, for once, too engrossed in her thoughts to look at the clock. She began to go round the class to see what work had been done. When she came to the last girl she stood up and gave an order.

'Time for the oral test. Shut your books please.'

Then she took a glance at the clock, and stared in surprise. Why, it was the end of the lesson already! How quickly the time had gone – but of course she had had to waste some of it waiting about for nothing in the common-room.

'Good gracious, look at the time!' she said. 'We can't have the oral test after all. Put away your books quickly please. Mam'zelle will be here in a moment.'

With grins of delight, and secret nudges, the girls put away their books quickly. Miss Roberts went out of the room to the fourth form, where she was due to give a maths lesson also. They were filled with surprise to see her arrive so early!

'Oh, Bobby, good for you! You've let us off that awful oral test!' said Alison. 'I do think you're a marvel!'

'Yes, you really are!' said Pat. 'It acted like clock-work. Wonderful!'

'Oh, it was nothing,' said Bobby, modestly, but secretly very thrilled at the admiration she was getting. Other girls loved to be praised for their work or their games – but Bobby revelled in admiration for her jokes and tricks!

Only Prudence again disapproved. 'Somehow it doesn't seem quite honest,' she said.

'Well, go and sneak about it to Miss Roberts then,' said Bobby at once. 'Little Miss Goody-Goody, aren't you? Where's your sense of fun?'

'What Prudence wants is a few jokes played on her,' said Janet. 'She's just too good to be true. Let's see if your wings are growing yet, Prudence!'

She pretended to feel down Prudence's thin back and the girl squirmed away angrily, for Janet's fingers were sharp. 'The budding angel,' said Janet. 'Tell me when you feel your wings sprouting, won't you?'

Miss Roberts was very much puzzled about the note and the fact that she was unexpectedly early for her next class. But this time she did not suspect a trick of any sort. She simply thought that some mistake had been made and dismissed it from her mind. She would never have thought of it again if Bobby and Janet, made bold by the success of the first trick, hadn't tried another of the same kind – far too soon!

# 6

# Janet in trouble

The girls were allowed to go down to the town together, either out to tea in a tea-shop, to the shops or to the cinema. No girl was allowed to go alone unless she was a top former. The younger ones loved to slip off together. They went to buy sweets, records, or cakes, and if there was anything good on at the cinema, it was fun to go.

That week there was a fine film being shown about Clive of India, and as the first form were then doing the same period with Miss Lewis in the history lesson, they all made up their minds to see it.

Miss Lewis encouraged them. 'You should certainly go,' she said. 'It will make your history lesson come alive for you. I will give a special prize to the best criticism written of the film by any first or second former.'

It was more difficult for the first form to go that week than for the second form. The first form had every afternoon full, and four of its evenings were taken up by meetings of some sort or other.

'I shan't be able to go until Friday,' sighed Janet. 'I've got to clean out the art cupboard for Miss Walker tonight, when most of you others are going. Oh, why did I offer to do it? The kindness of my heart runs away with me!'

'Well, it's not likely to run very far,' said Bobby. 'So cheer up!'

Janet threw a rubber at Bobby. They were in the common-room with the others, and there was a terrific noise going on. The radio was on at one end of the room, someone had set the record player going at the other, and Sheila and Kathleen were arguing at the tops of their voices about something.

'NEED we have both the radio AND the record player on together when nobody is listening to either?' pleaded Pamela's voice. 'I'm trying so hard to read and remember what I'm reading, and I simply can't.'

'Well, Pam, you shouldn't be working now,' said Pat, looking up from her knitting. 'You should slack off, like the rest of us. Why, you were saying history dates in your sleep last night, Sadie said!'

'Bobby, book me a seat for Friday night,' said Janet, looking everywhere for her rubber. 'I shall have an awful rush, I know, unless I can get Miss Roberts to let me off prep that night.'

'She let *me* off,' said Hilary. 'I went last night, and Miss Roberts was an awful brick – let me off half an hour early so that I could see the film.'

'Well, I'll ask her if she'll be a sport and let me off too,' said Janet. 'Oh blow, where *is* my rubber? Why did I throw it at Bobby? What a waste of a rubber!'

The next day was Thursday, and that evening the rest of the first form went to the cinema, except Janet, who kept her promise and turned out the untidy art cupboard for Miss Walker.

'I'll ask Miss Roberts to let me off early tomorrow,' thought Janet, as she threw all sorts of peculiar things out of the cupboard on to the floor. 'Golly, what a collection of things the art classes get! I don't believe this cupboard has been turned out for years!'

The next day Janet was unlucky. She had to do the flowers for the classroom that week, and Miss Roberts discovered that there was very little water in the vases. She looked disapprovingly at Janet.

'No wonder our flowers look sorry for themselves this week, Janet,' she said, poking a finger into the nearest vase. 'This bowl is almost empty. I do think you should attend to your responsibilities better, even the little ones.'

Janet flushed. Usually she was good at remembering small things as well as big, but the flowers had just slipped her memory that day. She muttered an apology and went to get a jug of water.

She came into the classroom with it, and was just about to pour water into a vase on the windowsill when the school cat jumped in at the window.

Janet was startled. She jumped violently and jerked the jug of water. A stream flew into the air – and landed very neatly on the back of Prudence's head! It dripped down her neck at once and the girl gave a loud squeal. Miss Roberts looked up, annoyed.

'What's the matter, Prudence? Janet, what have you done?'

'Oh, Miss Roberts! Janet has soaked me!' complained Prudence. 'She deliberately poured the water down my neck!'

'I didn't!' cried Janet. 'The cat sprang in through the window and made me jump, that's all.'

Miss Roberts eyed Janet coldly. She had seen too much of Janet's mischief to believe that it was entirely an accident.

'Prudence, go and dry yourself in the cloakroom,' she said. 'Janet, Prudence was engaged in writing out that list of geography facts for future reference. As she will not be able to finish it now, I would be glad if you would take her book and write the facts out for her during prep this evening.'

Janet stared in dismay, remembering that she had meant to ask for early leave. 'Miss Roberts, it really and truly was an accident,' she said. 'I'll write out what Prudence was doing, but may I do it in break, not in prep?'

'You will do it in prep,' said Miss Roberts. 'Now will you kindly finish playing about with that water and do a little work?'

Janet pursed up her lips and took the water out of the room. It looked as if she wouldn't be able to see the film now. As she went to the cloakroom to put away the jug, she met Prudence, who had dried herself quickly, for she was not really very wet.

'Prudence! You know jolly well it was a complete accident,' said Janet, stopping her. 'I want to leave prep early tonight, to see *Clive of India*. I shan't be able to unless you're decent and go and tell Miss Roberts you know it was an accident and ask her to let me off.'

'I shan't do anything of the sort,' said Prudence. 'You and Bobby are always playing silly tricks. I'm not going to get you out of trouble!'

She marched back to the classroom. Janet stared after her, angry and hurt. She stuck the jug back into the cupboard and slammed the door shut. Janet had a hot temper, and would willingly have poured a dozen jugs of icy-cold water all over Prudence at that moment!

When break came she told Bobby what had happened, and Bobby snorted in disgust. 'Prudence makes out she's so goody-goody,' she said, 'and yet she won't do a little thing like that. Now – let's see – is there any way of getting you off early to go to the film, Janet, in spite of everything?'

'No,' said Janet, dolefully. 'Miss Roberts is taking the first and second form together for prep tonight. If Miss Jenks was taking it I'd take a chance and slip out, hoping she wouldn't notice. But Miss Roberts will have her eye on me tonight.'

'I wonder – I just wonder – if I can't get Miss Roberts out of the room again,' said Bobby, her eyes beginning to gleam.

'Don't be an ass, Bobby,' said Janet, 'she can't be taken in twice that way – so soon after, too.'

'Well – what about doing it a bit differently?' said Bobby. 'Getting *you* called out, for instance?'

'Oooh,' said Janet, and her eyes danced. 'That *is* an idea! Yes – we might work it that way. But what about that beastly stuff I've got to write out for Prudence?'

'I'll do that for you,' said Bobby. 'I can make my writing like yours, in case Miss Roberts wants to see it.'

'All right,' said Janet. 'Well, now – how are we going to work it?'

'I'll ask Miss Roberts if I can go and fetch a book from the library,' said Bobby. 'And when I come back I'll say, "Please, Miss Roberts, Mam'zelle says can Janet go to her for some extra coaching?" And I bet Miss Roberts will let you go like a lamb – and you can slip off in time to see the whole of the picture.'

'It's a bit dangerous,' said Janet, 'but it's worth a try. Hope I shan't be caught.'

Don't-Care-Bobby grinned. 'Nothing venture, nothing have!' she said. 'Well, I'll do my best for you.'

So when the first and second form were all sitting quietly doing their prep that evening, Bobby put up her hand. 'Please, Miss Roberts, may I just slip along and get a book from the library?'

'Be quick, then,' said Miss Roberts, who was busy correcting books, and hardly looked up. Bobby grinned at Janet and slipped out of the room. She arrived back with a book under her arm and went to Miss Roberts's desk.

'Please, Miss Roberts, may Janet go to Mam'zelle now for a little extra coaching?' she said. Janet went red with excitement.

'Well,' said Miss Roberts, rather astonished, 'Mam'zelle didn't say anything to me about it when I saw her in the common-room. I suppose she forgot. Yes, Janet – you had better go – and you can write out those geography facts later on this evening, when you are in the first form common-room.'

'Thank you, Miss Roberts,' murmured Janet and scuttled out of the room like a rabbit. She rushed to the cloakroom, got her hat, flew out of the garden-door, went to the bicycle shed and was soon cycling down to the town as fast as she could go! How she hoped she would not meet any mistress or top former who would see that she was alone!

She slipped into the cinema unseen and was soon lost in the film, whilst the first form went on silently doing their prep for the next day. Only Prudence was suspicious, for she had seen the looks that passed between Janet and Bobby.

She was even more suspicious when she could not see Janet in the common-room that night, after prep. 'Janet is having a very long lesson with Mam'zelle,' she said to Bobby.

'Really?' said Bobby. 'How nice for them both!'

Bobby had copied out the geography for Prudence, trying to make her writing as like Janet's as possible. She laid the book down on Prudence's desk when the girl was out of the common-room for a minute. Prudence found it there when she came back. At first she thought Janet had written out the pages and she looked round for her. But Janet was still not there. How strange!

Prudence looked closely at her book. She saw that the writing was not really Janet's, and she stared at Bobby, who was lying in a chair, unconcernedly reading, her feet swung over the arm.

'This isn't Janet's writing,' said Prudence to Bobby. Bobby took no notice but went on reading. 'BOBBY! I said this isn't Janet's writing,' said Prudence, annoyed.

'Did you really say so?' said Bobby. 'Well, say it again if you like. I don't know if anyone is interested. I'm not.'

'I believe you and Janet made up a plot between you,' said Prudence, suddenly. 'I don't believe Mam'zelle wanted Janet at all – and I believe *you* wrote out these pages.'

'Shut up, I'm reading,' said Bobby. Prudence felt angry and spiteful. So Janet had managed to slip off to the cinema after all! Well, she would see that Miss Roberts knew it, anyway!

So the next morning, when Miss Roberts asked to see her geography book, to make sure that Janet had written out what she had been told, Prudence gave the game away. She went up to Miss Roberts's desk with her book and held it out. Miss Roberts gave a quick glance at it and nodded.

'All right!' she said, not noticing anything wrong with the writing.

'Bobby has written it out very nicely, hasn't she?' said Prudence, in a low, soft voice. Miss Roberts glanced sharply at the book and then at Prudence. She knew at once what the girl meant to tell her.

'You can go to your place,' she said to the girl, for she disliked sneaking. Prudence went, pleased that Miss Roberts had guessed what she meant.

Miss Roberts spoke to Mam'zelle when next she saw her. 'Did you by any chance give Janet Robins any extra coaching last night?' she asked. Mam'zelle lifted her eyebrows in astonishment.

'I was at the cinema,' she said. 'And so was Janet. I saw her! Why do you ask me such a question? I do not give coaching in the evenings.'

'Thank you,' said Miss Roberts, and beckoned to a passing girl.

'Go and find Janet Robins and ask her to come to me,' she said, grimly. The girl sped off and found Janet on the tennis-court.

'Wow!' said Janet when she got the message. 'Now I'm for it. The cat's out of the bag – but who let her out? Bobby, say goodbye to me for ever – I've got to face Miss Roberts in a rage – and I shan't come out alive!'

Bobby grinned. 'Poor old Janet!' she said. 'Good luck to you. I'll wait for you here, old thing.'

# 7

# Janet, Bobby – and Prudence

Janet went quickly to find Miss Roberts. When there was trouble brewing Janet faced up to it at once. She didn't run away from it, or make excuses. She wasn't looking forward to the interview with Miss Roberts, but she thought the sooner it was over the better.

Miss Roberts was in the first-form classroom correcting books. She looked up as Janet came in. Her face was very cold and stern.

'Come over here, Janet,' she said. Janet went to her desk. Miss Roberts finished correcting the book she had before her and then put down her pencil.

'So you didn't go to Mam'zelle for extra coaching last night?' she said.

'No, Miss Roberts, I didn't,' said Janet. 'I went to see *Clive of India* at the pictures. Bobby had booked me a seat the night before.'

'And who wrote out Prudence's geography lists then?' asked Miss Roberts.

'Well, Miss Roberts, I didn't,' said Janet after a pause. 'I – I can't tell tales.'

'I don't want you to tell tales,' said Miss Roberts. 'There is nothing that I detest more. I merely wanted to make sure you hadn't done the lists yourself.'

'I suppose Prudence split on me?' said Janet, her good-tempered face suddenly flushing.

'Well, I'm not telling tales either,' said Miss Roberts, 'but it won't be difficult for your own common sense to tell you how I found out about your gross disobedience. Janet, I'm not going to have you behaving like this. You have plenty of character, you are plucky, just and kind, though you have too quick a temper and too rough a tongue sometimes – but you and Roberta have got to pull yourselves together and realize that I am not here to play tricks on, but to make you work and really learn something. Especially this term, which should be your last one with me. I really feel ashamed of you.'

Janet went red again. She hated being scolded, but she knew it was just that she should be. She looked Miss Roberts straight in the face.

'I'm sorry,' she said. 'I didn't feel it was fair having to miss going to the cinema when I really didn't mean to spill that water on Prudence. It was a pure accident. If I'd done it deliberately, then I wouldn't have minded being punished.'

'You will leave it to me to judge whether or not a punishment is just,' said Miss Roberts, coldly. 'Now, as you used a bit of trickery to go down to the town last night, I feel you are not to be trusted for some time. You will not go down again unless you come to me, say why you want to go, and get my permission. Even so, I shall not grant any for a week or two. You will also do what I told you to do yesterday and write out the geography facts yourself – in Prudence's book as I said.'

'Oh, need I do it in her book?' said Janet in dismay. 'After all, the geography is already written out there once. Prudence will grin like anything if I go and ask her for her book.'

'You've brought it on yourself,' said Miss Roberts. 'And just remember this, my dear Janet – that much as I admire many things in your character, there is still plenty of improvement to be made – especially in your classwork. I feel very much inclined to go into the matter of that note I had the other day, which resulted in my leaving the maths class – it seems to me that that episode and this have a certain likeness that makes me feel very suspicious. Any more of that kind of thing from either you or Roberta will be instantly punished. Please tell Roberta this from me.'

'Yes, Miss Roberts,' said Janet, seeing from Miss Roberts's face that the teacher was in no mood to be generous or soft hearted. Miss Roberts hated being tricked, and usually prided herself on the fact that her first formers never *did* get the best of her. She was annoyed to think that her class might be laughing up their sleeves at her.

'You can go,' she said to Janet, and reached out for another book to correct. Janet hesitated. She badly wanted to get back into Miss Roberts's good books again, but somehow she felt this was no time to try and make amends. She must find a chance some other time, and bear her punishment as gracefully as she could.

She left the room and went gloomily back to the tennis-court, where Bobby was anxiously awaiting her. Bobby slipped her arm in Janet's.

'Was it very bad?' she asked, sympathetically.

'Beastly,' said Janet. 'I feel as small as that beetle on the grass down there. I can't go down to the town for a week or two, and after that I've got to go to Miss Roberts and beg for permission whenever I want to go. It's so humiliating. And oh, Bobby – I've got to write out those hateful geography lists again – in Prudence's book!'

'That's too bad,' said Bobby, feeling at once that Prudence would crow over Janet in delight. 'How did old Roberts find out about you?'

'There's only one way she could have,' said Janet, fiercely. 'That rotten Prudence must have split on me! I'll jolly well tell her what I think of her, that's all!'

The twins came up at that moment and heard with sympathy all that had happened to Janet. 'I heard that sneak of a Prudence say, "Bobby has written it out very nicely, hasn't she?" when she showed Miss Roberts one of her books this morning,' said Pat. 'I didn't know what she meant, of course. I just thought she was being nice about Bobby's writing. I didn't realize it was her horrid way of splitting on poor old Janet.'

'The beast!' said Bobby, her eyes flashing and her cheeks flaming. She was very fond of Janet. 'I'll pay her out all right! I'll make her squirm. The nasty little tell-tale. She always pretends to be so goody-goody too. I think she's a hypocrite. I'll go and get her beastly book for you,

Jan. You shan't have to go and do that, anyway – and if she dares to say a single word to me in that soft sneering way she has, I'll pay her back.'

'No, Bobby, don't do that,' said Janet. 'It's never any good to do things like that. Leave that to our Carlotta!'

Everyone grinned. Carlotta was a really fierce little creature when she was in a temper, and had berated Alison fiercely the day before, because Alison had pointed out that Carlotta's uniform was not tidy. Carlotta had listened with a wild expression on her face, and had then screamed at Alison, which had made Alison dissolve into tears.

'You find fault with me again, and you'll regret it!' threatened Carlotta.

'Carlotta, we don't behave like that here,' Hilary had said. 'Maybe you do in Spain – but you can't do it here; it just isn't right.'

Carlotta made a rude explosive sort of noise. 'Pah! If I want to shout, I shout! What right has this silly little peacock to talk about my uniform? See how she cries, the baby! She does not even argue back!'

Alison was not even thinking of such a thing. She was very hurt and upset, especially when Sadie Greene gave a laugh.

'My, Alison, you're just cat's-meat to that little savage! Cheer up. Don't you see she wanted to make you howl?'

The twins, Janet, and Bobby remembered this episode as they stood on the tennis-court listening to Bobby's suggestion that she should treat Prudence in the same way that Carlotta had treated Alison. They all knew that such things as screaming and threatening were out of the question! But nevertheless each one of them would dearly have loved to give Prudence a good scolding!

'It's what she wants,' said Pat, with a sigh. 'However – we'll see she's made to feel what a little beast she is, somehow. She won't get away with this.'

'I'll go and get the geography book from her,' said Bobby, and marched off. She went to the common-room, thinking that Prudence might be there. She was like Pam, always to be found indoors!

She was sitting doing a jigsaw puzzle. Bobby went up to her. 'Where's your geography book?' she said. 'I want it.'

'Oh, have you got to write something else in it?' said Prudence, in her clear, soft voice. 'Poor Bobby! Are you going to do it again for Janet? What will Miss Roberts say?'

'Look at me, you nasty little sneak!' said Bobby, in such a peculiar, threatening voice that Prudence was alarmed. She raised her eyes and looked at Bobby. Bobby was white with rage, and her eyes glinted angrily.

'You're going to be sorry for this,' said Bobby, still in the same peculiar voice, as if she was talking with her teeth clenched. 'I hate sneaks worse than anything. If you dare to tell tales again, I'll make you very sorry.'

Prudence was frightened. Without a word she got up, went to her shelf and fetched her geography book. She gave it to Bobby with a trembling hand. Bobby snatched it from her and went out of the room.

'I say!' said a small voice from the corner of the room. 'I say! Wasn't Bobby in a rage, Prudence? Whatever have you done?'

It was from Pam Boardman, curled up with a book as usual. She looked through her big glasses, her eyes very large.

'I've done nothing,' said Prudence. 'Nothing at all. I haven't sneaked or told any tales. But Bobby has got her knife into me because I think her tricks are a silly waste of time. Don't *you* think they are, Pam?'

'Well, I'm not very fond of games or jokes or tricks,' said Pamela. 'I've always liked my work better. But some of Bobby's jokes and Janet's do make me laugh. Still, I agree with Miss Roberts – if most of the first form have got to go up next term, tricks and things are a silly waste of time.'

'You're such a sensible girl, Pam,' said Prudence, going over to her. 'And so brainy, I wish you'd be my friend. I like you and Sadie better than anyone else in the form.'

Pam flushed with pleasure. She was a shy girl who found it very difficult to make friends, because she could not play games well, and found it impossible to think of funny things to say or do, as the others did. She did not see that Prudence wanted to make use of her.

'Of course I'll be friends,' she said, shyly.

'You've got such brains,' said Prudence, admiringly. 'I'd be so glad if you'd help me sometimes. I wish that Sadie would be friends with you too – it would do her good to think of something besides her hair and skin and nails. I like Sadie, don't you?'

'Well, I'm a bit afraid of her,' said Pam, honestly. 'She's got such grand clothes, and she does look so lovely sometimes, and she seems so very grown-up to me. I always feel small and dowdy when she comes along. I don't know whether I like her or not.'

Prudence tried to forget Bobby's unpleasant words to her, but it was difficult. She wondered what had happened. Had Miss Roberts made Janet write out those geography things all over again? What punishment would she give the girl?

When her book was returned to her, Prudence looked with curiosity inside the pages. Yes – there were the geography lists neatly written for the second time – this time in Janet's rather sprawly writing – and Miss Roberts had ticked it.

So she had to do it after all, thought Prudence. Good! Serves her jolly well right. Now perhaps she and Bobby will leave me alone for a bit, in case Miss Roberts gets after them again!

# 8

# Carlotta is surprising

The five new girls 'shook down' at St Clare's each in their
different ways. Sadie Greene sailed through the days,
taking no notice of anything except the things she was
really interested in. Miss Roberts's cold remarks passed
right over her head. Mam'zelle made no impression on
her at all. She thought her own thoughts, looked after her
appearance very carefully and took an interest in Alison
because the girl was really very pretty and dainty.

Prudence and Pam settled down too, though Prudence
was careful not to come up against Bobby and Janet more
than she could help. Bobby settled in so well that to the
old first formers it seemed as if she had belonged to St
Clare's for years. Carlotta too settled down in some sort
of fashion, though she was a bit of a mystery to the girls.

'She seems such a common little thing in most ways,'
said Pat, overhearing Carlotta talking to Pam in her curious
half-cockney, half-foreign voice. 'And she's so untidy and
hasn't any manners at all. Yet she's so natural and truthful
and outspoken that I can't help liking her. I'm sure she'll
come to blows with Mam'zelle some day! They just can't
bear each other!'

Mam'zelle was not having an easy time with the first

form that term. The girls who were to go up into the second form were not up to the standard she wanted them to be, and she was making them work very hard indeed, which they didn't like at all. Pam was excellent at French, though her accent was not too good. Sadie Greene was hopeless. She didn't care and she wasn't going to try! Prudence seemed to try her hardest but didn't do very well. Bobby was another one who didn't care – and as for Carlotta, she frankly detested poor Mam'zelle and was as nearly rude to her as she dared to be.

So Mam'zelle had a bad time. 'Do you wonder we called her "Mam'zelle Abominable" the first term we were here?' said Pat to Bobby. 'She has called you and your work "abominable" and "insupportable" about twenty times this morning, Bobby! And as for Carlotta, she has used up all the awful French names she knows on her! But I must say Carlotta deserves them! When she puts on that fierce scowl, and lets her curls drip all over her face, and screws up her mouth till her lips are white, she looks like a regular little tornado.'

Carlotta was really rather a surprising person. Sometimes she gave the impression that she was really doing her best to be good and to try hard – and then at other times it seemed as if she wasn't in the classroom at all! She was away somewhere else, dreaming of some other days, some other life. That would make Mam'zelle furious.

'Carlotta! What is there so interesting out of the window today?' Mam'zelle would inquire sarcastically. 'Ah – I see a cow in the distance? Is she so enthralling to you? Do you wait to hear her moo?'

'No,' Carlotta said, in a careless voice. 'I'm waiting to hear her bark, Mam'zelle.'

Then the class would chuckle and wait breathlessly for Mam'zelle's fury to descend on Carlotta's head.

It was in gym that Carlotta was really surprising. Since Margery Fenworthy had gone up into the second form, there had been nobody really good at gym left in the first form. Carlotta had done the climbing and jumping and running more or less as the others had done, though with less effort and with a curious suppleness – until one day in the third week of the term.

The girl had been restless all the morning. The sun had shone in at the classroom window, and a steady wind had been blowing up the hill. Carlotta could not seem to keep still, and paid no attention at all to the lessons. Miss Roberts had really thought the girl must be ill, and seriously wondered if she should send her to Matron to have her temperature taken. Carlotta's eyes were bright, and her cheeks were flushed.

'Carlotta! What *is* the matter with you this morning?' said Miss Roberts. 'You haven't finished a single sum. What are you dreaming about?'

'Horses,' said Carlotta at once. 'My own horse, Terry. It's a day for galloping far away.'

'Well, I think differently,' said Miss Roberts. 'I think it's a day for turning your attention to some of the work you leave undone, Carlotta! Pay attention to what I say!'

Fortunately for Carlotta the bell went for break at that

moment and the class was free to dismiss. After break it was gym. Carlotta worked off some of her restlessness in the playgrounds, but still had plenty left by the time the bell went for classes again.

Miss Wilton, the sports mistress, was gym mistress also. She had to call Carlotta to order several times because the girl would climb and jump out of turn, or do more than she was told to do. Carlotta sulked, her eyes glowing angrily.

'It is such silly baby stuff we do!' she said.

'Don't be stupid,' said Miss Wilton. 'You do most advanced things considering you are the lowest form. I suppose you think you could do all kinds of amazing things that nobody else could possibly do, Carlotta.'

'Yes, of course I could,' said Carlotta. And to the astonishment of the entire class the dark-eyed girl suddenly threw herself over and over, and performed a series of the most graceful cart-wheels that could be imagined! Round and round the gym she went, throwing herself over and over, first on her hands, then on her feet, as easily as any clown in a circus! The girls gasped to see her.

Miss Wilton was most astonished. 'That will do, Carlotta,' she said. 'You are certainly extremely good at cart-wheels – better than any girl I have known.'

'Watch me climb the ropes as they should be climbed!' said Carlotta, rather beside herself now that she saw the plain admiration and amazement in the eyes of everyone around. And before Miss Wilton could say yes or no, the little monkey had swung herself up a rope to the very top.

Then she turned herself completely upside-down there, and hung downwards by her knees, to Miss Wilton's complete horror.

'Carlotta! Come down at once. What you are doing is extremely dangerous!' ordered Miss Wilton, terrified that the girl would fall and break her neck. 'You are just showing off. Come down at once!'

Carlotta slid down like lightning, turned a double somersault, went round the gym on hands and feet again and then leapt lightly upright. Her eyes shone and her cheeks were blazing. It was plain that she had enjoyed it all thoroughly.

The girls gazed open-mouthed. They thought Carlotta was marvellous, and every one of them wished that she could do as Carlotta had done. Miss Wilton was just as surprised as the girls. She stared at Carlotta and hardly knew what to say.

'Shall I show you something else?' said Carlotta, breathlessly. 'Shall I show you how I can walk upside-down? Watch me!'

'That's enough, Carlotta,' said Miss Wilton in a firm voice. 'It's time the others did something! You certainly are very supple and very clever – but I think on the whole it would be best if you did the same as the others, and didn't break out into these odd performances.'

The gym class went on its usual way, but the girls could hardly keep their eyes off Carlotta, hoping she would do something else extraordinary. But the girl seemed to sink into her dreams again, and scarcely looked at anyone else.

After the class was over the girls pressed round her.

'Carlotta! Show us what you can do! Walk on your hands, upside-down.'

But Carlotta wasn't in the mood for anything more. She pushed her way through the admiring girls, and suddenly looked rather depressed.

'I said I wouldn't – and I have,' she muttered to herself, and disappeared into the passage. The girls looked at one another.

'Did you hear what she said?' said Pat. 'I wonder what she meant. Wasn't she marvellous?'

It seemed to have done Carlotta good. She was much better in her next classes after her curious performance in the gym, quieter and happier. She lost her scowl and was not at all rude to Mam'zelle in French conversation.

The girls begged her to perform again when the gym was empty, but she wouldn't. 'No,' she said. 'No. Don't ask me to.'

'Carlotta, wherever did you learn all that?' asked Isabel, curiously. 'You did all those things just as well as any clown or acrobat in a circus! The way you shinned up that rope! We always thought Margery Fenworthy was marvellous – but you're far better!'

'Perhaps Carlotta has relations who belong to a circus,' said Prudence, maliciously. She didn't like the admiration and attention suddenly given to the girl, and she was jealous. She thought Carlotta was common and she wanted to hurt her.

'Shut up, Prudence,' said Bobby. 'Sometimes you make

67

me think how lovely it would be to teach you a lesson.'

Prudence flushed angrily. The other girls grinned. They liked seeing Prudence taken down a peg or two.

'Come on to the tennis-court,' said Pat to Bobby, seeing that a quarrel was about to begin. 'We've got to practise our serving, Miss Wilton said. Let me serve twenty balls to you, and you serve back to me. Next month there are going to be matches against St Christopher's and Oakdene, and I jolly well want to be in the team from the first form.'

'Well, I'll come and let you practise on *me*,' said Bobby, with a last glare at Prudence, 'but it's not a bit of good me hoping to be in any tennis team. Come on. Let's leave old Sour Milk behind.'

How Prudence hated that name! But whenever she made one of her unkind remarks, someone was sure to whisper 'Sour Milk'. Prudence would look round quickly, but everyone would look most innocent, as if they hadn't said a single word.

Prudence hated Bobby because she had begun the nickname, but she was afraid of her. She would dearly have loved to give Bobby a clever, unkind name too – but she couldn't think of one. And in any case Bobby was 'Bobby' to the whole school. Even the mistresses presently ceased calling her Roberta, and gave her her nickname. Much to Prudence's anger, Bobby was one of the most popular girls in the form!

# 9

# Prudence makes a discovery

Two or three quite exciting things happened during the
next week or two, and all of them had to do with Carlotta.
The first happened at the swimming-pool. Carlotta was
no swimmer, but she adored diving and jumping. She
was excellent on the spring-board too, which jutted out
over the water.

Most of the girls could run lightly along the board and
dive off the end of it – but Carlotta could do far more than
that! She could run along it, leap high into the air, turn
two or three somersaults and land in the water with her
body curled up into a ball – splash! She could stand at
the end of the board, bounce herself up and down till the
board almost touched the water, and then with one last
enormous bounce send herself like a stone from a catapult
into the air, turning over and diving in beautifully as she
came down.

She jumped or dived from the topmost diving
platform, and she came down the water-chute in every
possible position, even standing, which was a quite
impossible feat for any other girl. Her swimming was
always peculiar, but for acrobatic feats in the water no
one could possibly beat Carlotta.

She didn't show off. She did all these things perfectly naturally, and with the utmost enjoyment. Prudence, who was a bad swimmer and disliked the water, never joined in the general praise and admiration that the other girls gave to Carlotta.

'She's just showing off,' Prudence said in a loud scornful voice, as Carlotta did a beautiful somersault into the water near her. Prudence herself was shivering at the top of the steps, not yet having gone in. The water was cold that morning, and courage was not Prudence's strong point. Alison was beside her, also shivering.

'She's not showing off,' said Janet, who overheard what Prudence said. 'It's just natural to her to do all those things. You're jealous, my dear Prue! What about going down another step and getting your knees wet? You've been shivering there for the last five minutes.'

Prudence took no notice of Janet. Carlotta climbed up to the topmost diving platform and did a graceful swallow dive that made even Miss Wilton clap in admiration.

'There she goes, showing off again,' said Prudence, talking to Alison. 'Why people encourage her I can't imagine. She's conceited enough as it is.'

'That's just the one thing Carlotta isn't,' said Bobby. 'Hold that horrid tongue of yours, Prudence. It's difficult to believe you were brought up in a vicarage when we hear you talk like that.'

'Well, it's quite plain our dear Carlotta was not brought up in any vicarage,' said Prudence, spitefully. Carlotta overheard this and grinned. She never seemed to mind remarks of this sort, though it made the others angry for her when Prudence said them. Bobby pursed up her mouth and looked at Prudence's white shivering back with distaste.

'What about a dip, dear Prue?' she said suddenly, and gave the girl a violent push. Into the pool went the surprised Prue with a loud squeal. She came up angry and spluttering. She looked round for Bobby, but Bobby had dived in immediately behind her and was now under the water groping for Prudence's legs!

In half a second Prudence felt somebody getting tight hold of the calf of her left leg and pulling her under the water! Down she went with another agonized squeal and disappeared below the surface, gasping and spluttering. She came up again, almost bursting for breath – but no sooner had she got her wind again than once more Bobby caught hold of her leg and pulled her under.

Prudence struggled away and made for the side of the pool at once, calling to Miss Wilton.

'Miss Wilton, oh, Miss Wilton, Bobby is almost drowning me! Miss Wilton, call Bobby out!'

Miss Wilton looked round in surprise at the yells from Prudence. Bobby by this time had got to the other end of the pool and was almost dying of laughter.

'What do you mean, saying that Bobby is drowning you?' said Miss Wilton, impatiently. 'Bobby's right at the other end of the pool. Don't be an idiot, Prudence. Pull yourself together and try to do a little swimming. You seem to spend most of your time standing on the steps like a scared three-year-old.'

There were a few titters from the girls nearby. Prudence was so angry that she fell back into the water and swallowed about two pints all at once.

'I'll pay you out for that!' she called to Bobby, but Bobby merely waved her hand and grinned.

'Perhaps you'll keep your tongue off Carlotta a bit if you think you're going to have Bobby after you for it!' remarked Janet, who was nearby, enjoying the fun.

Prudence unburdened her mind to Pamela Boardman as they walked back to the school building that afternoon. 'It's so bad for that common little Carlotta to have us all staring at her open-mouthed, and thinking she's wonderful,' said Prudence. 'I don't see why people like Carlotta should be allowed to come to a good school like this, do you, Pam? I mean, it's not fair on girls like us, is it, who come of good families and have been well brought up? Why, Carlotta might have a very bad influence on us indeed.'

'Perhaps her parents think that we might have a good influence on Carlotta?' suggested Pam, in her soft voice. 'She *is* odd, I agree – but she's quite fun, Prudence.'

'I don't think the things she does are really clever,' said Prudence, spitefully. 'I don't think she's fun, either. I think there's a decided mystery about our Carlotta – and I'd dearly like to know what it is!'

Pam was younger than Prudence, and although she was a clever girl at her work, she was very easily influenced by Prudence. Soon she was agreeing to all that the older girl said, and even when Prudence said things that were plainly untrue and unkind about others, Pam listened to her respectfully and nodded her head.

It was Pam and Prudence who discovered Carlotta doing something extraordinary, not long after the episode at the swimming-pool. The two of them were going for a nature-walk together, taking with them their notebooks and their nature specimen cases. They set off over the hill and went across the fields that lay behind the school. The country swept upwards again after a little, and big fields lay behind high hedges. It was a beautiful day for a walk, and Pam, who seldom went out, was quite enjoying herself.

Prudence would not have gone out at all for a walk if she hadn't seen Carlotta making off by herself. The girls were not allowed to go out alone, unless they were top formers, and two or three times Prudence had suspected that Carlotta was disobeying the rules.

Today she had seen Carlotta slipping off through the school grounds to the little gate that was set in the garden wall a good way behind the school. Prudence had been in the dormitory, and her sharp eyes picked out the girl at once. 'I wonder what she does when she goes off alone,' thought Prudence, spitefully. 'Where does she go? I bet she's got some common town friends that nobody knows anything about. I'd like to follow her and find out.'

Prudence was cunning. She knew it would be no good to go to Pam Boardman and suggest spying on Carlotta because Pam, though having a great respect for Prudence, shied away from anything underhand. So Prudence ran downstairs and found Pam curled up as usual, reading.

'Hallo, Pam!' she cried. 'Let's go out for a nature-walk! The fields look lovely behind the school this afternoon. Do come with me. It will do you good.'

Pam was good natured. She shut up her book and went to get her hat and notebook. The two girls set off. Down through the grounds they went, out of the gate and then across the field paths. Prudence kept a sharp look-out for Carlotta, and soon caught sight of the figure in the school blazer, a good way off, going up the hill opposite.

'I wonder who that is,' she said carelessly to Pam. 'We'll keep her in sight and perhaps join up with her on our way home.'

'We can't do that,' said Pam. 'She's alone so it must be one of the top formers. She wouldn't want to walk home with *us*!'

'Oh, I forgot that,' said Prudence. 'Well, we may as well go the same way as she does. She probably knows the right paths.'

So the two girls kept Carlotta in sight. The girl made her way over the top of the hill and then down into the next valley. Here there was a big camp, for a circus had come to the next town. In a vast field many caravans and cages were arranged, and in the centre an enormous tent towered up.

'There must be a circus at Trenton,' said Prudence. 'But Carlotta can't be going to it, because the show won't be on now.'

'How do you know it's Carlotta?' said Pam, in surprise.

'It can't be! She's not allowed out by herself. However *can* you tell who it is so far away?'

Prudence was annoyed with herself. She hadn't meant to let Pam know she knew it was Carlotta. 'Oh, I've got wonderful eyesight,' she said. 'You have to wear glasses, so probably your eyes don't see as far as mine. But I'm pretty sure it's Carlotta. Isn't that just like her – slipping out and breaking the rules?'

'Yes, it is rather like her,' said Pam who, however, could not help rather admiring the fiery little girl for her complete disregard of rules and regulations when she wanted to do something very badly. Carlotta always went straight for a thing, riding over objections and obstacles as if they were not there.

They followed Carlotta to the big field. They saw her speak to an untidy-haired, rough-looking groom. He smiled at Carlotta and nodded. The girl left him and went into the next field where there were some beautiful circus horses. In half a minute the girl had caught one, leapt on to its back and was galloping round the field, riding beautifully, although it was bareback.

Pam and Prudence stared in the utmost surprise. Whatever Prudence had imagined Carlotta might be going to do she certainly hadn't thought of this! She could hardly believe her eyes. The two girls watched Carlotta on the beautiful horse, which first galloped swiftly round the field, and then fell to a canter. The man she had spoken to came to watch her. He called out something to her and pointed to another horse. This was more the cart-horse type, broad backed and staid.

Carlotta called something back to the man. She leapt off her horse and ran to the one he had pointed out to her. In a trice she was up on its back, calling to it. It began to run round the field.

And then Carlotta did something that made the two hidden girls gape even more! She stood up on the horse's back and, keeping her balance perfectly, made the horse trot round and round as if it were in a circus ring! Prudence's mouth shut in a straight line.

'I always thought there was something strange about Carlotta,' she said to Pam. 'Now we know what it is. I'm sure she's nothing but a jumped-up circus-girl. How *could* Miss Theobald have her here? It's wicked! Whatever will the others say?'

'Don't let's sneak, Prudence,' begged Pam, timidly. 'Please don't. This is Carlotta's secret, not ours. We'd better say nothing.'

'Well, we'll bide our time,' said Prudence, in a spiteful voice. 'We'll just bide our time. Come on – we'd better get back before she sees us watching.'

So the two girls made their way back to the school, mostly in silence. Prudence was gloating because she had discovered something so peculiar about Carlotta – and Pam was puzzled and worried, fearful that Prudence would give away Carlotta's secret, and drag her, Pam, into the unpleasantness too. They arrived back at school just in time for tea.

Pat and Isabel saw them going indoors and called to

them in surprise. 'I say! You don't mean to say you two have actually been for a nature-walk! I thought neither of you could be dragged out of doors!'

'We had a *lovely* walk,' said Prudence, 'and we saw some very interesting things.'

'What have you brought back, Pam?' asked Hilary, seeing that Pam had her nature-specimen case slung over her shoulder.

Pam flushed. She had nothing, and neither had Prudence. It seemed as if the whole walk had been nothing but following Carlotta, spying on her, and then thinking about her all the way back. Prudence certainly hadn't spoken a word about nature, and Pam hadn't liked to ask her to stop when she saw anything that she herself was interested in.

Prudence saw that Pam was uncomfortable because they had brought nothing back for the nature-class. So she lied glibly.

'We've heaps of things,' she said. 'We'll keep them till after tea. We're hungry now – and there's the tea bell.'

Prudence knew that no one would be interested enough to ask to see any nature specimens after tea. She pushed Pam in the direction of the cloakroom, so that they might wash their hands.

Pam was silent as she washed. She was a truthful person herself, and it puzzled her when Prudence told fibs, for the girl was always condemning others who did wrong – and yet here she was lying quite cheerfully!

'Perhaps it was because she didn't want to say we'd seen

Carlotta,' said Pam to herself. 'She was just shielding her.'

Carlotta arrived late for tea. She muttered an apology to Miss Roberts and sat down. She was red with running, and although she had brushed her unruly dark curls, she looked untidy and hot.

'Wherever have you been, Carlotta?' said Pat. 'I looked all over the place for you this afternoon. It was your turn to play tennis. Didn't you know?'

'I forgot,' said Carlotta, taking a piece of bread and butter. 'I went out for a walk.'

'Who with?' said Janet.

'By myself,' said Carlotta, honestly, lowering her voice so that Miss Roberts could not hear. 'I know it's breaking the rules – but I couldn't help it. I wanted to be by myself.'

'You'll get caught one of these days, you monkey,' said Bobby. 'I break a good few of the rules myself at times – but you seem to act as if there weren't any at all. You be careful, Carlotta!'

But Carlotta only grinned. She had a secret which she meant to keep to herself. She didn't know that somebody else found it out!

# 10

# An uproar in Mam'zelle's class!

The next thing that happened was an uproar in Mam'zelle's French class. The term was getting on, and many of the first formers seemed to have made no progress in French at all. The weather was very hot just then, and most of the girls felt it and were disinclined to work hard. Girls like Pam Boardman and Hilary Wentworth, both of whom had brains, a steady outlook on their work, and a determination to get on, worked just as well as ever – but the twins slacked, and as for Sadie and Bobby, they were the despair of all the teachers.

But it was Carlotta who roused Mam'zelle's anger the most. When Carlotta disliked anyone she did not hide it. Neither did she hide her *liking* for any girl or teacher – she would do anything for a person she liked. The twins, and Janet and Bobby, found her generous and kind, willing to do anything to help them. But she thoroughly disliked Alison, Sadie, Prudence, and one or two others.

Carlotta's idea of showing her dislike for anyone was childish. She would make faces, turn her back, even slap. She would stamp her foot, call rude names, and often lapse into some foreign language, letting it flow out in an angry stream from her crimson lips. The girls rather enjoyed all this, though Hilary, as head of the form, often took the girl to task.

'Carlotta, you let yourself down when you act like this,' she said, after a scene in which Carlotta had called Alison and Sadie a string of extraordinary names. 'You let your parents down too. We are all more or less what our parents have made us, you know, and we want them to be proud of us. Don't let your people down.'

Carlotta turned away with a toss of her head. 'I don't let my parents down!' she said. 'They've let *me* down. I wouldn't stay here if I hadn't made a promise to someone. Do you suppose I would ever choose to be in a place where I had to see people like Alison and Sadie and Prudence every day? Pah!'

The girl almost spat in her rage. She was trembling, and Hilary hardly knew what else to say.

'We can't like everyone,' she said at last. 'You *do* like some of us, Carlotta, and we like you. But can't you see that you only make things worse for yourself when you act like this? When you live in a community together, you have to behave as the others do. I'm head of the form, and I just can't let you go around behaving like a four-year-old. After all, you are fifteen.'

Carlotta's rage vanished as suddenly as it had appeared. She genuinely liked the steady responsible Hilary. She put out her hand to her.

'I know you're right, Hilary,' she said. 'But I haven't been brought up in the same way as you have – I haven't learnt the same things. Don't dislike me because I'm different.'

'Idiot!' said Hilary, giving her a clap on the shoulder. 'We like you because you *are* so different. You're a most exciting person to have in the form. But don't play into the hands of people like Prudence, who will run to Miss Roberts if you bring out some of your rude names. If you really want to let off steam, let it off on people like me or Bobby, who won't mind!'

'That's just it,' said Carlotta. 'I *can't* go for you – you're too decent to me. Hilary, I'll try to be calmer. I really will. I'm getting on a bit better with Miss Roberts now – but Mam'zelle always drives me into a rage. I'll have to be extra careful in her class.'

It was Bobby who really began the great uproar in Mam'zelle's class one morning. Bobby was bored. She hated French verbs, which had an irritating way of having different endings in their past tenses. Just as if it was done on purpose to muddle us, thought Bobby, with irritation. And I never can remember when to use this stupid subjunctive. Ugh!

Nearby Bobby was a vivarium, kept by the first formers. It was a big cage-like structure, with a glass front that could be slipped up and down. In it lived a couple of large frogs and a clumsy toad. With them lived six large snails. The first formers regarded these creatures with varying ideas.

Kathleen, who loved animals, was really attached to the frogs and toad, and vowed she could tell the difference between the six snails, which she had named after some of the dwarfs in the story of Snow White. The rest of the form could only recognize Dopey, who never seemed to move, and who had a white mark on the spiral of his shell.

The twins liked the frogs and toad, and Isabel often tickled the frog down his back with a straw because she liked to see him put his front foot round, with its funny little fingers, and scratch himself. Some of the class were merely interested in the creatures, the rest loathed them.

Sadie and Alison couldn't bear them, and Prudence shuddered every time she saw the frogs or toad move. Doris disliked them intensely too. Bobby neither liked nor disliked them, but she had no fear of the harmless creatures as Prudence and the others seemed to have, and she handled them fearlessly when their vivarium needed to be cleaned or rearranged.

On this morning Bobby was bored. The French class seemed to have been going on for hours, and seemed likely to continue for hours too, though actually it was only a lesson lasting three-quarters of an hour. A movement in the vivarium caught the girl's eye.

One of the frogs had flicked out its tongue at a fly that had ventured in through the perforated zinc window at the back. Bobby took a quick look at Mam'zelle. She was writing French sentences on the blackboard, quite engrossed in her task. The girls were supposed to be reading a page of French, ready to translate it when she was ready.

Bobby nudged Janet. Janet looked up. 'Watch me!' whispered Bobby with a grin. Bobby slid the glass front of the vivarium to the back and put in her hand. She took one of the surprised frogs out and then shut the glass lid.

'Let's set him hopping off to Prudence!' whispered Bobby. 'It'll give her an awful fright!'

No one else had noticed Bobby's performance. Mam'zelle was irritable that morning, and the class were feverishly reading over their page of French, anxious not to annoy her more than they could help. Bobby reached over to set the frog on Prudence's desk.

But the poor creature leapt violently out of her hands on to the floor near Carlotta. The girl caught the movement and turned. She saw the frog on the floor, and Bobby nodding and pointing to show her that it was meant for the unsuspecting Prudence.

Carlotta grinned. She had been just as bored as Bobby in the French class, and the page of French had meant nothing to her at all. She hardly understood one word of it.

She picked up the frog and deposited it neatly on the edge of Prudence's desk. The girl sat next to her, so it was easy. Prudence looked up, saw the frog and gave such a scream that the whole class jumped in fright.

Mam'zelle dropped her chalk and the book she was holding, and turned round with an angry glare.

'PRUDENCE! What is this noise?'

The frog liked Prudence's desk. It hopped over her book and sat in the middle of it, staring with unwinking brown eyes at the horrified girl. She screamed loudly again and seemed quite unable to move. She was really terrified.

The frog took a leap into the air, and landed on Prudence's shoulder. It slipped down to her lap, and she leapt up in horror, shaking it off.

'Mam'zelle! It's the frog! Ugh, I can't bear it, I can't bear it! Oh, you beast, Carlotta! You took it out of the vivarium on purpose to give me a fright! How I hate you!' cried Prudence, quite beside herself with rage and fright.

Most of the class were laughing by now, for Prudence's horror was funny to watch. Mam'zelle began to lose her temper. The frog leapt once more and Prudence screamed again.

'*Taisez-vous*, Prudence!' cried Mam'zelle. 'Be silent. This class is a garden of bears and monkeys. I will not have it. It is *abominable*!'

More giggles greeted this outburst. Prudence turned on Carlotta again and spoke to her with great malice in her voice.

'You hateful creature! Nothing but a nasty little circus girl with circus-girl ideas! Oh, you think I don't know things about you, but I do! I saw you take the frog out of the vivarium to make him leap on me. I saw you!'

'*TAISEZ-VOUS*, Prudence,' almost shouted Mam'zelle, rapping on her desk. 'Carlotta, leave the room. You will go straight to Miss Theobald and report what you have done. That such things should happen in my class! It is not to be believed!'

Carlotta did not hear a word Mam'zelle said. She had sprung up from her seat and was glaring at Prudence. Her eyes were flashing, and she looked very wild and very beautiful. Like a beautiful warrior, Isabel thought.

She began to speak – but not one of the girls could understand a word, for Carlotta spoke in Spanish. The words came pouring out like a torrent, and Carlotta stamped her foot and shook her fist in Prudence's face. Prudence shrank back, afraid. Mam'zelle, furious at being entirely disregarded by Carlotta, advanced on her with a heavy tread.

The whole class watched the scene, breathless. There had been one or two Big Rows, as they were called, in the first form at times, but nothing to equal this. Mam'zelle took Carlotta firmly by the arm.

'*Vous êtes in-sup-por-table!*' she said, separating the syllables of the word to make it even more emphatic. Carlotta shook off Mam'zelle's hand in a fury. She could not bear to be touched when she was in a rage. She turned on the astonished French mistress, and addressed her in a flow of violent Spanish, some of which Mam'zelle unfortunately understood. The mistress went pale with anger, and with difficulty prevented herself from giving Carlotta a box on the ears.

In the middle of this the door opened and Miss Roberts came in. It was time for the lesson to end, but everyone had been far too engrossed in the scene to think of the time. Miss Roberts had been surprised to find the classroom door shut, as usually it was held open for her coming by one of the class. She was even more astonished to walk in and see Mam'zelle and Carlotta apparently about to have a free fight!

Mam'zelle recovered herself a little when she saw Miss Roberts. 'Ah, Miss Roberts!' she said, her voice quite weak with all the emotion she had felt during the last few minutes. 'You come in good time! This class of yours is shocking – yes, most shocking and wicked. That girl Carlotta, she has defied me, she has called me names, she has – oh la, la, there is the frog again!'

Everyone had forgotten the frog – but it now made a most unexpected appearance again and leapt on to Mam'zelle's large foot. Mam'zelle had no liking for frogs. All insects and small creatures filled her with horror. She gave a squeal and stumbled backwards, falling heavily on to a chair.

Miss Roberts had taken everything in at a glance. Her face was extremely stern. She looked at Mam'zelle. She knew Mam'zelle's hot temper, and she felt that the best thing to do was to get the angry French mistress out of the class before making any inquiries herself.

'Mam'zelle, your next class is waiting for you,' she said in her clear cool tones. 'I will look into this matter for you and report to you at dinner-time. You had better go now and leave me to deal with everything.'

Mam'zelle could never bear to be late for any class. She got up at once and left the room, giving Carlotta one look of fury before she went. Miss Roberts nodded to Hilary to shut the door and then went to her own desk. There was a dead silence in the room, for there was not a girl there who did not dread Miss Roberts when she was in this kind of mood.

Carlotta was still standing, her hair rumpled over her forehead, her fists clenched. Miss Roberts glanced at her. She knew Carlotta's fiery nature by now, and felt that it was of no use at all to attack her in that mood. She spoke to her firmly and coldly.

'Carlotta, please go and do your hair. Wash your inky hands too.'

The girl stared at her teacher, half mutinous, but the direct order calmed her and she obeyed it. She left the room and there was a sigh of relief. Carlotta was exciting – but this time she had been a little *too* exciting.

'Now please understand that I am not encouraging any tale-bearing,' said Miss Roberts, looking round her class with cold blue eyes, 'but I am going to insist on finding out what this extraordinary scene is about. Perhaps you, Hilary, as head of the class, can tell me.'

'Miss Roberts, let *me* tell you!' began Prudence, eager to get her word in before anyone else. 'Carlotta opened the vivarium and took out the frog, and . . .'

'I don't want any information from you until I ask for it, Prudence,' said Miss Roberts, in such a cutting tone that the girl sank back into her seat, flushing. 'Now, Hilary – tell me as shortly as you can.'

'Well, apparently someone took a frog out of the vivarium and put it on Prudence's desk,' said Hilary reluctantly. Bobby got up, red in the face.

'Excuse me interrupting, Miss Roberts,' she said. '*I* took the frog out.'

'It was that beast Carlotta who played the trick on me!' exclaimed Prudence. 'You're shielding her.'

'Prudence, you'll leave the room if you speak again,' said Miss Roberts. 'Go on, Bobby.'

'I was bored,' said Bobby, honestly. 'I took out the frog to make it jump on to Prudence for a bit of fun, because she's scared of frogs. But it leapt out of my hand on to the floor – and so I nodded to Carlotta to pick it up and put it on the desk – and she did. But I was the one to blame.'

Bobby sat down. 'Now you go on with this extraordinary tale, Hilary,' said Miss Roberts, wondering if her class could really be in its right senses that morning.

'Well, Miss Roberts, there isn't much else to tell except that Prudence got an awful fright and screamed and Mam'zelle was angry, and Prudence blamed it all on to Carlotta and said some pretty horrid things to her, and Carlotta flared up as she does – and when Mam'zelle ordered her from the room she wouldn't go – I really think she didn't even *hear* Mam'zelle! Then Mam'zelle was furious because Carlotta didn't obey her and went over to her – and Carlotta turned on her and said something in Spanish that made Mam'zelle even more furious. And then you came in,' finished Hilary.

'And spoilt your fun, I suppose,' said Miss Roberts in the sarcastic voice that the class hated. 'A very entertaining French lesson, I must say. You appear to have begun it all, Bobby – Carlotta certainly had a hand in it –

and the rest of the tale appears to be composed of bad tempers on the part of several people. I imagine that everyone was simply delighted, and watched with bated breath. I'm disgusted and ashamed. Bobby, come to me at the end of the morning.'

'Yes, Miss Roberts,' said Bobby, dismally. Prudence looked round at Bobby with a pleased expression, delighted that the girl had a punishment coming to her. Miss Roberts caught sight of the look. She could not bear Prudence's meanness, nor her habit of tale-bearing and gloating over others' misfortunes. She snapped at her so suddenly that Prudence jumped.

'Prudence! You are not without blame, either! If you *can* make trouble for others, you invariably do. If you had not made such a stupid fuss none of this would have happened.'

Prudence was deeply hurt. 'Oh, Miss Roberts,' she said, in an injured tone, 'that's not fair. Really I . . .'

'Since when have I allowed you to tell me what is fair and what is not?' inquired Miss Roberts. 'Hold your tongue and sit down. And while I think of it – your last essay was so bad that I cannot pass it. You will do it again this evening.'

Prudence flushed. She knew that Miss Roberts definitely meant to be unkind at that moment, and she felt that all the girls, except perhaps Pam, silently approved of Miss Roberts's sharp tongue, and were pleased at her ticking-off. Her thoughts turned to Carlotta, and she brooded with bitterness over the fiery girl and what she had said. Miss Roberts had said nothing about punishing that beast Carlotta! Surely she wasn't going to let her go scot-free! Think of the things she had said to Mam'zelle! Carlotta was strange and bad – see how she broke the rules of the school and went off riding other people's horses!

The class was in a subdued mood for the rest of that morning. Bobby went to Miss Roberts and received such a scolding that she almost burst into tears – a thing that Bobby had not done for years! She also received a punishment that kept her busy for a whole week – a punishment consisting of writing out and learning all the things that Miss Roberts unaccountably appeared to think that Bobby didn't know. It is safe to say that at the end of that week Bobby knew a good deal more than at the beginning!

Carlotta appeared to receive no punishment at all, which caused Prudence much anger and annoyance. Actually, as Pat and Isabel knew, Carlotta had been sent to the head, Miss Theobald, and had come out of that dread sitting-room in tears, looking very subdued and unlike herself. She told no one what had passed there, and nobody dared to inquire.

Mam'zelle received a written apology from Bobby and from Carlotta – and, much to Prudence's anger, one from Prudence herself too! Miss Roberts had demanded it, and would not listen to any objections on Prudence's part. So the girl had not dared to disobey but had written out her apology too.

I'll pay Carlotta out for this! she thought. I'll go and

find that man she was talking to – and ask him all about that horrid beast of a Carlotta! I'm sure there's something funny about her.

# 11

## Carlotta's secret

The first chance that Prudence had of going for a walk over to the circus camp was two days later. She sought out Pam and asked her to go with her.

'Oh, Prudence! I did so badly want to finish reading this book,' said Pam, who was in the middle of a historical novel dealing with the class's period of history. It was quite a joke with the first form that Pam never read any book unless it had to do with some of the classwork.

'Pam, do come,' begged Prudence, slipping her hand under Pam's arm. Pam had had very little affection shown to her in her life and she was always easily moved by any gesture on Prudence's part. She got up at once, her short-sighted eyes beaming behind their big glasses. She put away her book and got her hat. The two girls set off, going the same way as before.

In half an hour's time they reached the camp. 'Why, we've come the same way that we came last week!' said Pam.

'Yes,' said Prudence, pretending to be astonished too. 'And look – the circus camp is still there – and those lovely horses are still in the field. Let's go down to the camp and see if we can see any elephants or exciting things like that.'

Pam wasn't at all sure that she wanted to find

elephants, for she was nervous of animals, but she obediently followed Prudence. They went into the field where the caravans and cages were arranged. No one took any notice of them.

After a while Prudence's sharp eyes found the untidy-haired man that she had seen Carlotta talking to. She went up to him.

'Does it matter us looking round the camp a bit?' she asked, with her sweetest smile.

'No, you go where you like, missy,' said the man.

'Are those the circus horses in that field over there?' asked Prudence, pointing to the field where she had seen Carlotta riding.

'They are,' said the man, and he went on polishing the harness that lay across his knees.

'I wish we could ride them like Carlotta,' said Prudence, gazing at the horses with an innocent expression. The man looked at her sharply.

'Ay, she's a fine rider,' he said. 'Fine girl altogether, I say.'

'Have you known her long then?' said Prudence, still looking very innocent indeed.

'Since she was a baby,' said the man.

'She's had an awfully interesting life, hasn't she?' said Prudence, pretending that she knew far more than she did. 'I love to hear all her stories.'

Pam stared at Prudence open-mouthed. This was news to her! She wondered uncomfortably if Prudence was telling one of her fibs – but why should she do that?

'Oh, she's told you about her life, has she?' said the

man, looking rather surprised. 'I thought she wasn't . . .'

He stopped short. Prudence felt excited. She really was discovering something now. She looked at the untidy man, her eyes wide open with a most honest expression in them. No one could beat Prudence at looking innocent when she wasn't!

'Yes, I'm her best friend,' said Prudence. 'She told me to come over here and look round the camp. She said you wouldn't mind.'

Pam was now quite certain that Prudence was telling dreadful untruths. In great discomfort the girl went off to look at a nearby caravan. She felt that she could not listen any more. She could not imagine what Prudence was acting like this for. She had so little spite in her own nature that it did not occur to her to think that Prudence was trying to find out something that might damage Carlotta.

Prudence was pleased to see Pam go off. Now she could get on more quickly! She felt certain somehow that Carlotta really had been connected with circus life in some way, so she took the plunge and asked the man the question.

'I expect Carlotta loved circus life, didn't she?'

The man apparently saw nothing odd about the question. He plainly thought that Carlotta had told Prudence a great deal about herself. He nodded his head.

'She oughtn't to have left it,' he said. 'My brother, who was in the same show as Carlotta was, said it would break her heart. That girl knew how to handle horses better than a man. I was glad to let her have a gallop when she came over here the other day. We move tomorrow – so you tell her when you get back that if she wants another gallop, she'll have to come along pretty early tomorrow morning, like she did two weeks ago.'

Prudence was almost trembling with excitement. She had found out all she wanted to know. That nasty little Carlotta was a circus girl – a horrid, common, low-down little circus girl! How dare Miss Theobald accept a girl like that for her school! Did she really expect girls like Prudence, daughter of a good family, to mix with circus girls?

She called Pam and the two set off to go back to the school. Both were silent. Pam was still feeling very uncomfortable about Prudence's untruths to the man in the camp – and Prudence was thinking how clever she had been. She did not realize that it was not real cleverness – only shameful cunning.

She wondered how she could get the news round among the girls. Should she drop a hint here and there? If she could get hold of that foolish Alison, she would soon bleat it out everywhere! She went to find Alison that evening in the common-room. The girl was sitting doing a complicated jigsaw. She loved jigsaws, although she was very bad at them, and usually ended in losing half the pieces on the floor.

It was an interesting jigsaw. Four or five girls came to see how Alison was getting on. Bobby picked up a piece.

'Doesn't that go there?' she said, and tried it. Then

Hilary picked up another piece, and in trying to make it fit, pushed the half-finished picture crooked.

'Oh!' cried Alison, exasperated. 'If there's one thing I hate more than anything else it's having people help me with a jigsaw puzzle. First it's Bobby, then it's Hilary, then it's somebody else. I could finish it much more quickly if only people didn't help me!'

'I've never seen you finish a jigsaw puzzle yet, Alison,' said Pat, teasingly.

'Why don't you do it properly?' said Doris who, however poor she was at lessons, was astonishingly quick at jigsaws. 'You always begin by putting little bits together here and there. What you should do is begin with the outside pieces. You see, they've got a straight edge, and . . .'

'I know all that,' said Alison, impatiently, 'but Sadie says . . .'

Immediately the chorus was taken up with the greatest delight by the girls around.

'Sadie says – oh, Sadie says – Sadie, Sadie, Sadie SAYS!'

The girls at the back of the room took up the chorus too, and Sadie good-naturedly lifted her pretty head. 'Don't you mind them, Alison,' she said. But Alison did. She never could take teasing well. She muddled up her half-made jigsaw in peevishness, piled it into its box, dropped two or three pieces on the floor and went out of the room.

Prudence followed her, thinking she might drop a few words into Alison's ear. 'Alison!' she called. 'What a shame to tease you like that! Come out into the garden with me. It's a lovely evening.'

'No, thanks,' said Alison, half rudely, for she did not like Prudence. 'I'm not in the mood to hear nasty things about half the girls in the form!'

Prudence flushed. It was true that she lost no chance of telling tales about the girls, trying to spread mischief among them – but she had not realized that the girls themselves knew it. It was plainly no use trying to get Alison to listen to tales about Carlotta.

'I'll have to think of some other way,' said Prudence to herself. But she did not have to think – for the whole thing came out that same evening far more quickly than Prudence had ever expected.

She went back into the common-room. Carlotta was there, laughing as she told some joke in her half-foreign voice, which was rather fascinating to listen to. The girls were grouped around her, and Prudence felt a sharp twinge of jealousy as she saw them.

Her face was so sour as she looked at Carlotta that Bobby laughed loudly. 'Here comes old Sour Milk!' she said, and everyone giggled.

'Sour Milk!' said Carlotta. 'That is a very good name. Why have you gone sour, Prudence?'

Prudence was suddenly full of spite. 'It's enough to make anyone go sour when they have to live with a low-down circus girl like you!' she said, her tone so full of hate that the girls glanced at her in astonishment. Carlotta laughed.

'I'd like to see *you* in a circus!' she said cheerfully. 'The tigers would like you for their dinner. And I don't believe anyone would miss you.'

'Be careful, Carlotta,' said Prudence. 'I know all about you. All – about – you!'

'How interesting!' said Carlotta, though her eyes began to gleam dangerously.

'Yes – very interesting,' said Prudence. 'The girls would soon despise you if they knew what I know. You wouldn't have any friends then. No one would want to know – a common little circus girl!'

'Shut up, Prudence,' said Bobby, afraid that Carlotta might lose her temper. 'Don't tell silly lies.'

'It's not silly lies,' said Prudence. 'It's the truth, the whole truth. There's a circus camp over near Trenton, and I talked to a man there – and he told me Carlotta was a circus girl, and knew how to handle horses, and was nothing but a common little girl from a circus belonging to his brother. And *we* have to put up with living with a girl like her!'

There was a complete silence when Prudence had finished. Carlotta looked all round the girls with flashing eyes. They stared at her. Then Pat spoke.

'Carlotta – did you *really* live in a circus?'

Prudence watched everyone, pleased with her bombshell. Now Carlotta would see what decent, well-brought-up girls would say to her. She, Prudence, would have a fine revenge. She waited impatiently for the downfall of the fiery little Carlotta.

At Pat's question Carlotta looked towards the twins.

She nodded her head. 'Yes,' she said. 'I *was* a circus girl. And I loved it.'

The girls looked in amazement and delight at Carlotta. Her eyes were glowing and her cheeks were red. They could all imagine her quite well riding in a circus ring. They pressed round her eagerly.

'Carlotta! How marvellous!'

'I say, Carlotta! How simply wonderful!'

'Carlotta, you simply *must* tell us all about it!'

'I always knew there was something unusual about you.'

'Oh, Carlotta, to think you never told us! Why didn't you, you wretch?'

'Well – I promised Miss Theobald I wouldn't,' said Carlotta. 'You see – it's a funny story really – my father married a circus girl – and she ran away from him, taking me with her, when I was a baby. She died soon after, and I was brought up by the circus folk. They were grand to me.'

She stopped, remembering many things. 'Go on,' said Kathleen, impatiently. 'Do go on!'

'Well – I loved horses, just as my mother did,' said Carlotta, 'so I naturally rode in the ring. Well, not long ago, my father, who'd been trying to find me and my mother for years, suddenly discovered that mother was dead and I was in a circus. Father is a rich man – and he made me leave the circus, and when he found how little education I'd had he thought he would send me to school to learn.'

'Oh, Carlotta – how awfully romantic!' said Alison. 'Just like a book. I always thought you looked unusual,

Carlotta. But why are you so foreign?'

'My mother was Spanish,' said Carlotta, 'and some of the folk in the circus were Spanish too, though many of them came from other parts of Europe! They were grand people. I wish I could go back to them. I don't fit in here. I don't belong. I don't think like you do. Our ideas are all different – and I'll never never learn.'

She looked so woe-begone that the girls wanted to comfort her.

'Don't you worry, Carlotta! You'll soon fit in – better than ever now we know all about you. Why didn't Miss Theobald want us to know you'd been a circus girl?'

'Well, I suppose she thought maybe you might look down on me a bit,' said Carlotta. The girls snorted.

'Look down on you! We're thrilled! Carlotta, show us some of the things you can do!'

'I promised Miss Theobald I wouldn't do any of my tricks,' said Carlotta, 'in case I gave the show away. I broke my promise the other day in the gym – but somehow I simply couldn't help it. I'd been thinking and dreaming of all the old circus days – and of my darling beautiful horse, Terry – and I just went mad and did all those things in the gym. I can do much more than I showed you then!'

'Carlotta! Walk on your hands upside-down!' begged Bobby. 'Golly! What fun you're going to be! You're a fierce creature with your fly-away tempers and ready tongue – but you're natural and kind and we shall all like you even better now we understand the kind of life you've lived before. It's a wonder you've fitted in as well as you did.

What a mercy you were honest about it – we wouldn't have admired you nearly so much if you'd been afraid to own up.'

'Afraid to own up – why, I'm proud of it!' said Carlotta, with sparkling eyes. 'Why should I be ashamed of knowing how to handle horses? Why should I be ashamed of living with simple people who have the kindest hearts in the world?'

The girl threw herself lightly over and stood on her hands. Her skirt fell over her shoulders as she began to walk solemnly round the room on her strong, supple little hands. The girls crowded round her, laughing and admiring.

'My word – the second form will be jealous when they hear about Carlotta!' said Bobby.

'They certainly will!' said Sadie, who was just as full of astonishment and admiration as anyone else. It all seemed most surprising and unreal.

Everyone was pleased and thrilled – save for one girl. That girl, of course, was Prudence. She could not understand the attitude of the girls. It was completely opposite to what she had expected. It was hard to believe.

Prudence stood in silence, listening to the squeals of delight and admiration. Her heart was very bitter within her. The bombshell she had thrown had certainly exploded – but the only person it had harmed had been the thrower! Instead of making the girls despise Carlotta and avoid her, she had only succeeded in making them admire her and crowd round her in delight. Now Carlotta would show off even more – she would get more friends than ever. How could everyone like a nasty common little girl like that?

No one took any notice of Prudence. For one thing they were so excited about Carlotta – and for another thing they despised her for her mean attempt to injure another girl for something she couldn't help. Bobby elbowed her a little roughly, and Prudence almost burst into tears of rage and defeat.

She slipped out of the room. It was more than she could bear to see Carlotta walking on her hands, cheered on by the rest of the first formers. The last words she heard were, 'Let's get the second formers in! Where are they? In the gym? Do let's go and tell them to come and see Carlotta! She's marvellous!'

I meant my news to hurt her – and it's only brought her good luck and friendship, thought Prudence bitterly. Whatever shall I do about it?

# 12

# Bobby gets a shock

Carlotta was a very popular person after this upheaval. Her complete honesty and frankness had disarmed everyone, and to most of the girls she suddenly appeared as a most surprising and romantic person. Even the second formers were thrilled, though as a rule they professed rather to turn up their noses at anything that happened in the first form. But Tessie, Queenie and the rest of the second form were just as persistent as the lower form in begging Carlotta to show off her circus tricks and accomplishments.

'It must have been a bit of a shock to that sneak of a Prudence to find that instead of looking down on our Carlotta we looked up to her and admired her instead!' said Pat. 'I bet dear darling Prudence thought we'd be shocked to the back teeth to hear she was a circus girl. I vote we punish her by not taking a scrap of notice of her, and not listening to anything she says!'

'I think we ought to do the same to Pam then,' said Bobby. 'Pam's Prudence's friend, you know, and she was with her when they spied on Carlotta. She's a silly little creature and thinks the world of Prudence. It will do her good to feel that we don't approve of Prudence's ways, and don't particularly want to be pleasant to Prudence's friends.'

'Well, I'm rather sorry for Pam,' said Isabel. 'She's a nervous little thing and awfully hard working. Don't let's be too hard on her.'

Prudence didn't at all like the treatment meted out to her by the first formers. The girl was very fond of the sound of her own voice, and it was most annoying to her to find that whenever she began to air her views about anything, all the girls around either suddenly disappeared, or else began to talk nonsense to one another at the tops of their voices.

Prudence would perhaps address herself to Hilary and say, 'Hilary, what side are you taking in tonight's debate on "Should Women rule the World?" I'm taking the side that they certainly should. After all, don't we . . .'

Then Hilary would suddenly address Janet in a very loud voice and say something perfectly ridiculous, such as, 'I say, Janet, old thing, how many legs has a kitten?'

And Janet, perfectly solemn, would answer in a loud voice, 'Well, usually four. But you'd better count and see.'

Prudence would stare in astonishment, and then begin again. 'What I say is, if women ruled the world . . .'

Then Kathleen would chime in, cutting right across Prudence's rather affected little voice. 'Hilary, Janet! Do you suppose a worm really grows into two worms when it's cut in half?'

Then Bobby would cut in, rather cruelly. 'What about cutting dear Prudence in two, then we'll see!'

And so it went on, nobody ever paying any attention to Prudence at all. Prudence was hurt and angry and went to Pam for comfort. She squeezed out a few tears and Pam tried to comfort her.

'Pam, you know quite well I wasn't spying on Carlotta,' wept Prudence. 'Can't you tell the girls I wasn't? Do stick up for me. What's the good of being my friend if you don't?'

And then poor Pam, trying her hardest to be loyal, would stick up for Prudence, although in her heart of hearts she no longer really trusted or liked her. But the thirteen-year-old girl was easily swayed, and anyone in tears moved her heart.

So it came about that very soon the first formers began to ignore poor Pam too, and laughed at her efforts to stick up for Prudence. Pam retired into her shell and felt very unhappy. She worried about the whole thing and turned to her work more than ever to help her to forget the many unpleasantnesses that seemed to be cropping up in those weeks.

Now that her secret was out, Carlotta was very happy. Hers was an honest nature, and she had not liked keeping everything to herself. Now the whole school knew what she was and eyed her with wonder, half expecting her to do something extraordinary at any time. The twins took her under their wing, and they and Carlotta, Bobby and Janet were continually about together.

Carlotta had gone to Miss Theobald and had told her that everyone now knew she had once been a circus girl.

'But they don't seem to mind,' said Carlotta, looking straight at the head mistress with her fearless eyes. 'You thought they would, didn't you?'

'No, Carlotta, I didn't think that most of them would mind at all,' said Miss Theobald. 'But I thought it might be easier for you to settle down if the girls did not regard you as anything out of the ordinary. Also your father begged me to keep your "secret" as he called it. Well – it's out now – and you must just show me that it doesn't matter. You are all your father has, you know – so try and get used to the kind of life you will have to lead with him later on.'

Carlotta sighed. She didn't want to lead any other kind of life except the one she had always known – the life of the circus camp, always on the move, always visiting new places, always making new friends. She left Miss Theobald's sitting-room looking rather subdued.

After a while the excitement caused by the row in Mam'zelle's class, and by Carlotta's secret, died down a little. This was partly because matches were looming ahead – tennis and swimming – and the school was putting in a good deal of practice, hoping to win all the matches against other schools.

The twins were practising hard, and Bobby was helping them. Don't-Care Bobby would not do anything much to help herself on, but never minded how much time she gave to help anyone else to become better at anything. Janet and Hilary were both practising too, but were not so good as the twins.

'You're getting a grand style at tennis, both of you,'

said Belinda Towers, approvingly, as she watched the twins one afternoon. 'If you go on like this you'll be chosen for the first-form team against St Christopher's! Bobby, you're getting better too. Why don't you try a bit harder and see if you can't be the reserve girl?'

Two out of each form were chosen to play against two girls from each form of the opposing school, and for each two there was a reserve girl, in case one of the two fell ill or could not play for any other reason. Bobby shook her head when she heard Belinda say this.

'No, thanks!' she said. 'It makes tennis too much like hard work if I have to practise up for reserve girl!'

Belinda was not amused by this answer. She gave Bobby a look that rather surprised her, because it held a certain amount of scorn in it.

'Oh, well,' said Belinda, 'of course we can't expect Don't-Care Bobby to care enough for the school, or to have enough pride in her form to do anything that might seem like hard work. Foolish of me to suggest it!'

She walked away and the three stared after her. 'What's bitten *her* this afternoon?' said Bobby, surprised. The twins looked at her uncomfortably.

'Well, Bobby, I suppose it must seem to the top girls that you do just what you like and don't bother about working or playing as hard as you might,' said Pat, at last. 'Mind you, I'm not blaming you, not one bit – I think you're grand as you are – but the top formers have other ideas about things. You know how good and proper they get as they go up the school. Maybe one day *you'll* be good and proper too – though I jolly well hope you won't!'

'Don't worry, I shan't,' said Bobby, shortly. She hadn't at all liked what Belinda had said. She wondered if she ought to put in a bit of hard practice at tennis herself, just to please Belinda. But she was obstinate and didn't, though she went on helping the twins all she could, standing at the other end of the court for a long time whilst they served ball after ball across the net, trying to improve their style.

Sadie, Alison, Pam, Prudence, and Carlotta made no pretence at all of trying to better their tennis. They either played because they had to, or because there wasn't anything better to do at the moment. Not one of the five, with the exception of Carlotta, visited the swimming-pool except on the days when it was compulsory to do so. These days came three times a week, and how Prudence and Sadie groaned when they had to go down to the pool and undress themselves, shivering, in the little wooden cubicles that ran alongside the water.

Carlotta was quite mad in the water, for although she could not swim well or fast, she performed all sorts of antics there, and her diving was lovely to watch. Miss Wilton hardly knew what to make of her.

'You'll never make a swimmer, Carlotta,' she said, 'but I shouldn't be surprised if you take all the prizes for your tricks! That was a lovely swallow-dive you did just now. But please don't come down the chute standing up any more. It's dangerous. And also, do try *not* to jump into the water from the top of the diving platform just when

Prudence is underneath. You scare her terribly.'

'Oh, Miss Wilton, I wouldn't scare Prudence for worlds!' said Carlotta, in her up-and-down voice, and a wicked look in her eyes. And the very next moment she ran along the marble floor, pretended to slip, and landed with an enormous splash in the water, right on top of the unfortunate Prudence! No one ever knew what Carlotta would do next.

The twins hoped against hope that they would be chosen to play against St Christopher's. It would be such fun to play together. 'Won't Mummy be pleased if she hears we've both been chosen?' said Pat. 'I wish Bobby could be our reserve girl and come with us. But I bet Janet or Hilary will be chosen.'

The match was to be the following week, and three girls from each of the three lower forms were to go to St Christopher's School for the matches against girls from similar forms there. Belinda promised to put up the names of the girls on the board the night before.

Before Belinda put up the names, she sent for Bobby. Bobby went to Belinda's study in surprise. The big girl was there, neatly writing out some sports lists.

'Hallo, Bobby,' she said, nodding her head towards a chair. 'Sit down for a minute. I've nearly finished.'

Bobby sat down and studied Belinda's clear-cut profile. She liked Belinda very much, and knew how hard she worked at being sports captain. She wondered what Belinda was going to say to her.

The sports captain looked up and set down her pen.

'Look here, Bobby,' she said, 'I just want to know something. You're pretty good at tennis, and I'd half-thought of making you reserve girl for your form. But I want to know if you've been thinking about it too, and working for it.'

'No, I haven't,' said Bobby, going red. 'I told you that that would be too much like hard work, Belinda! Anyway, reserve girls never play in the matches – they only watch – and I don't want to watch! If I was going to do anything, I'd want to play, not watch!'

'You're very disappointing,' said Belinda. 'You've got such good stuff in you, Bobby – but you won't seem to make the best of it. I believe if you'd practised as hard as the twins, I'd not have known who to choose for the two match players! You put yourself out to let Pat and Isabel practise all they like on you – but yet you won't try to make yourself good too. Don't-Care Bobby is a good name for you – but you won't get far if you don't begin to care about things.'

'I don't want to get far,' said Bobby, her obstinacy rising. 'I've told you, Belinda – I'd like to *play* in the match – but I'm not keen on watching – so choose Janet or Hilary for reserve girl. I don't care!'

'Very well,' said Belinda, coldly. 'I shall choose one of the others. I was hoping you would be able to tell me you really had done a bit of hard practising on your own account – then I would certainly have chosen you for reserve girl – but seeing that you don't seem to care either way, I shall choose somebody else. You can go.'

Bobby went out of the room, red of cheek, and rather

ashamed of herself. She was an odd mixture. She had plenty of brains, plenty of high spirits, plenty of kindliness – but she seemed to have an incurable dislike of working hard at anything, and if anyone tried to make her, she became very obstinate and immovable. Belinda felt really impatient with her.

The sports captain made out the list of three girls chosen for the tennis match next day, and went to pin it on the noticeboard. A crowd came round her immediately.

'Pat! Isabel! You're the two girls!' yelled Doris at the top of her voice. 'Who's reserve girl? Take your fat head out of the way, Prudence!'

The reserve girl was Janet. She was delighted. She turned to Bobby. 'I thought it would be *you*,' she said. 'You're much better than I am, really. I can't think why Belinda chose me instead of you, Bobby!'

Bobby knew quite well, but she said nothing. She was cross because she couldn't help feeling ashamed of herself. 'I'm jolly glad it's you, old girl,' she said to Janet. 'Reserve girls never play – we all know that – but you'll have some fun, anyway!'

# 13

# Three tennis matches – and an accident

The next day dawned warm and sunny – just right for a tennis match. There was a little breeze, but not enough to worry the players. The match was to start at three o'clock. The nine girls chosen – three from each of the three lower forms – were to go with Belinda and Miss Wilton in a small private bus that the school often used.

Pat and Isabel were in a great state of excitement. They had not played for their school before, and were proud and pleased.

'Isn't it lovely that we're to play *together*?' said Pat joyfully. 'It would have been horrid if one of us had been chosen and not the other.'

Janet was almost as excited as they were, because although she was only reserve girl and hadn't a chance in a hundred of really playing, still it was great fun to go off in the bus to another school. She and the other two reserve girls would be able to sit with Belinda Towers and Miss Wilton and talk with them whilst the game was on.

'Good luck!' said everyone, when the little bus drew up to the school door and the tennis players went to get in. 'Good luck! Mind you win *all* the matches! We'll give you three hearty cheers when you come back, if you do! Good luck!'

Bobby felt a little envious as she saw the happy faces of the twins and Janet smiling in the bus. She knew she herself might have been in that bus if she had really wanted to! But nobody guessed her thoughts, for she shouted 'Good luck!' and waved as wildly as the rest.

It was fun to go driving through the countryside to St Christopher's like that. The girls fingered the strings of their rackets and looked at them anxiously to make sure they were all tight and good. Their tennis shoes shone as white as snow. Their tennis-whites were spotless. They all hoped they would make a good showing in the matches against the opposing school.

They arrived at the school, and were met by the sports captain there, a tall graceful girl in white, and by the girls who were to play against them. They all went to the sports ground, chattering hard.

'Our courts badly want a little rain,' said a St Christopher's girl. 'The service lines are getting very worn. We've hard courts as well as grass ones, but we thought we'd use the grass ones today because they are so much softer to the feet – and also there's more room round our grass courts for the school to watch. We want everyone to see us giving you St Clare girls a beating! You beat us last year, so it's our turn this year!'

Margery Fenworthy was one of the second formers chosen, and she was eager to begin. She was wonderful at all games, and had been practising hard in order to perfect her tennis style. Her friend, Lucy Oriell, had been chosen as her partner, and both girls were delighted. Lucy was inclined to work far too hard, and Margery had made her take as much recreation as possible – and now, here was Lucy, her dark curls dancing round her face, happy at having a whole afternoon away from her scholarship work.

Jane Rickson and Winnie Hill were the third formers chosen. All six St Clare players changed into their tennis shoes and took off their cardigans.

'We thought, as you are nice and early, we would play all three matches separately, instead of at the same time,' said the St Christopher's sports captain. 'The third formers could play first. Are you ready? Will you toss for sides, please? Smooth or rough!'

Jane Rickson and Winnie Hill won the toss and chose the side. The match was to be the best of three sets. The players took their places. Jane was serving. She threw the ball high into the air – and the match began!

It was really exciting to watch. The two sets of partners were very evenly matched, and the games were very close. Practically all of them ran up to deuce. The first set was won by St Clare's, seven-five. The second one was won by St Christopher's, six-four.

'And now for the third set!' said Pat, excitedly. 'Gosh, aren't Jane and Winnie playing well, Belinda? Do you think they'll win?'

'I rather think they will,' said Belinda, smiling at

Pat's eager face. 'The other two seem to me to be getting a little tired.'

Belinda was right. The St Christopher's girls were not now so fresh as the St Clare's two. All the same the last set was very close and very exciting, and went to five all. Then Jane won her serve straight off. Six-five!

'Play up, Jane and Winnie!' yelled the twins. 'Play up!'

And they played up! They skipped about the court, they hit every ball, they smashed the gentle balls and killed the hard ones – and lo and behold, St Clare's had won the first match, two sets to one!

'Match to St Clare's, two sets to one,' called the umpire. 'Good game, everybody!'

St Christopher's cheered the winners. The girls shook hands across the net, and then went to drink long drinks of sweet lemonade with bits of ice bobbing at the top. How good it tasted!

'Golly, that was a good match,' panted Jane, stretching her long, tired body out over the grass. 'Look – there go the next lot. Play up, Margery. Play up, Lucy! Belinda, I don't think there's any doubt about *this* match, do you? I think Margery and Lucy will just wipe the floor with the St Christopher's girls.'

'I shall be very surprised indeed if our two don't win, I must say,' said Belinda. 'I'm jolly pleased *you* two managed to pull it off. There wasn't much in it, you know – but you and Winnie managed to keep a bit fresher. It was fine to see you skipping about like that in the last game. Well done!'

There was never any doubt at all about the result of the second match. Lucy and Margery had it all their own way. The two girls opposing them were very good indeed – but Margery played a marvellous game. She and Lucy made perfect partners, never leaving any part of the court unprotected. Margery won all her serves outright.

'Golly, she's good,' said Belinda. '*Isn't* she good, Miss Wilton?'

'Marvellous,' said the St Clare's sports mistress. 'And how happy she looks too. Quite different from the sulky Margery we had to deal with last term!'

The twins remembered what a sullen, bad-tempered girl Margery Fenworthy had been the term before, and then how her whole outlook had been changed when she had become a heroine in one night, through rescuing another girl in a fire at the sickbay. Now here was that same Margery, winning honours for her school, as proud of St Clare's as St Clare's was proud of her!

The match was over in two sets. 'Match to St Clare's,' called the umpire, 'won outright in two sets, six-one, six-love.'

'Now it's our turn!' said Pat to Isabel, in great excitement, as she watched the second-form girls shaking hands across the net. 'Come on, Isabel. We've just GOT to win!'

'Play a steady game, twins,' said Belinda. 'You *ought* to win. You play almost as well together as Margery and Lucy. My word, how terribly proud St Clare's would be of us if we went back tonight having won all three matches! We simply MUST!'

The twins leapt to their feet, and ran on to the tennis-court, rackets in hand. 'Call for sides!' cried the St Christopher's girl, and twisted her racket.

'Rough!' called Pat, and 'rough' it was. Pat chose the side, and the four took up their places. Belinda was pleased to see how steady the twins were. They had practised continually together, and were almost as good partners to one another as Margery and Lucy.

They won the first three games, lost one and won another. And then a dreadful thing happened!

Pat was serving. The ball came back to the left-hand side of Isabel and swerved away unexpectedly. The girl swung herself round to hit it, twisted her ankle and fell over, crashing quite heavily to the ground. She immediately tried to get up but her foot gave way beneath her and she fell again with a surprised cry of pain.

Pat rushed over to her anxiously. 'Isabel! What's happened? Oh, *don't* say you've twisted your ankle!'

'I'll be all right in a minute,' said Isabel, her face rather pale, for her foot hurt her very much. 'Just wait a minute till the pain goes off.'

But the pain didn't go off, and it was not long before the ankle swelled up tremendously. 'You've strained it,' said Miss Wilton. 'Twisted it badly, I'm afraid. Poor old Isabel – what bad luck! I'll have to take you off the court and get Janet to take your place.'

And so it came about that for once the reserve girl *did* play! But alas for poor Janet – the sight of Isabel looking so woe-begone and pale quite upset her, and made her thoroughly nervous. She felt that at any costs she and Pat must win – but somehow she couldn't play as well as she hoped.

For one thing she hadn't practised a great deal with either of the twins, and hadn't learnt how to play a good partnership game. She would keep rushing to Pat's court, leaving her own unguarded, so that her opponent found it easy to place a ball where Janet could not get it. And when Pat went up to the net Janet forgot to run to the back-line, so that balls went over her head and she could not get them.

They lost the first set, four-six – and alas, they lost the second, four-six also. They were very sad and disappointed.

'Cheer up,' said Belinda, as they came off the court. 'You both look like Sour-Milk Prudence! It couldn't be helped.'

'You'd have won if Isabel had been able to play with you,' said Janet to Pat. 'And I believe you'd have won if Bobby had been the reserve girl and not me. Bobby hasn't any nerves at all – she would just have stepped right into Isabel's place, and played magnificently. She always comes up to scratch when she has to. And she's practised with you so often that she knows your game better than I do. She'd have made a much better partner. Belinda, don't you think so?'

'Well,' said Belinda, honestly, 'I agree that Bobby knows Pat's game better than you do – but all the same I'm not sure she'd have won the match.'

But Pat and Isabel, Janet and the others were sure!

They talked about it as they ate a good tea, and discussed it in the bus on the way home.

The St Clare's girls were delighted to hear that the third and second forms had won their matches, and were sorry over poor Isabel's fall. Her ankle had now gone down a little, and was feeling very much better.

'It will be all right in a day or two,' said Matron when she examined it. 'Bad luck, Isabel! Just the wrong time to have a fall, in the middle of a most important match!'

Isabel smiled wanly. She had been most bitterly disappointed about the whole thing, especially when she had seen Pat lose the match to the St Christopher's girls. She poured out her disappointment to Bobby.

'Bobby, I believe Pat would have won if only Belinda had chosen *you* for reserve girl instead of Janet!' she said. 'Janet did her best – but she isn't as used to Pat's game as you are. Oh, why didn't Belinda choose *you*? I do think that was a great mistake on her part. If you'd played in the match Pat and you would have won it, and then St Clare's would have won all three!'

Bobby listened in silence. She knew quite well why Belinda hadn't chosen her! She had been silly and obstinate. She had let St Clare's down! She felt sure she wouldn't have been so nervous as Janet, and she *did* know Pat's style of game very well indeed.

She was so silent that Isabel was astonished. 'What's up, Bobby?' she said. 'You look awfully glum. You don't mind as much as all that about the match being lost, do you?'

'Yes, I do,' said Bobby. 'It wasn't Belinda's fault that Janet was chosen instead of me. Belinda did give me the chance – and I didn't take it. Don't blame Belinda. Blame me. You heard what Belinda said to me on the courts the other day – well I was sore and angry about it, and I just got all obstinate and thought I jolly well wouldn't do what she said and work hard at my tennis.'

'What a pity, Bobby,' said Isabel. 'You could have been reserve girl – and you weren't!'

'Yes – Belinda sent for me last night,' said poor Bobby. 'I missed my chance – and the match was lost. I don't say I could have won it with Pat any more than Janet could – but I can't get rid of the horrid feeling that I might have – and then think how pleased everyone would have been if we'd won all three matches. I thought I didn't care about anything, so long as I had a good time and did what I wanted to. But I find I do care after all!'

She went off by herself, for once in a way looking unhappy. Poor Bobby! She wasn't really as don't-carish as she pretended to be!

# 14

# Bobby and the squeaking biscuit

The term went on, passed the half-way mark, and slipped into full summer. It was wonderful weather and the girls thoroughly enjoyed everything – except having to work so hard with Miss Roberts and Mam'zelle!

'Bobby, can't you possibly think of something to stop Mam'zelle making us recite French verbs this morning?' said Pat, with a groan. 'I *have* learnt them – but they all slip out of my head with this lovely summer weather. Just think of a little tiny trick to take Mam'zelle's attention off verbs for even five minutes.'

'You haven't played a trick on anyone for at least a week!' said Isabel.

'Bobby's gone all serious,' laughed Janet.

Bobby smiled. She had certainly turned over a new leaf in some ways, for she had suddenly begun to practise both her tennis and her swimming very hard indeed. She had swum underwater for the whole length of the swimming-pool, and everyone had clapped her. She had even tried diving, which as a rule she avoided because she so often dived in flat on her stomach, and hurt herself.

But although she was working hard at games, she still did as little as she possibly could in class. Miss Roberts looked grim sometimes, when she eyed Bobby. She knew quite well that the girl was not using her good brains to the utmost – but as neither sarcastic remarks nor punishments seemed to move Don't-Care Bobby to work harder, the teacher had almost given her up.

The girls around Bobby went on begging her to play some kind of joke on Mam'zelle to make the French class a little easier that day.

'Mam'zelle's in an awful temper this morning,' said Doris. 'The second form said she almost threw the blackboard chalk at Tessie because she sneezed seven times without stopping.'

The twins grinned. They knew Tessie's famous sneezes. It was quite an accomplishment of Tessie's – she had the ability to sneeze most realistically whenever she wanted to. She often used this gift to relieve the second form from boredom. All the teachers suspected that Tessie's sneezes were not at all necessary, but only Miss Jenks knew how to deal with them properly.

'Tessie! Another cold coming!' she would say. 'Go straight to Matron and ask her to give you a dose out of Bottle Number Three, please.'

Bottle Number Three contained some very nasty-tasting medicine indeed. Tessie could never make up her mind whether it was a concoction specially made up for her, or really was medicine reserved for possible colds. So she used her sneezes rather sparingly in Miss Jenks's presence – but gave Mam'zelle the full benefit of them whenever she could.

This particular morning she had given seven very explosive sneezes, making Mam'zelle nearly jump out of her skin, and reducing the class to a state of helpless giggling. Mam'zelle had been very angry – and all the other classes expecting her to teach them that morning knew they would be in for a bad time.

'If you don't think of some trick or other to play, Mam'zelle will keep our noses to the grindstone every minute of the lesson,' groaned Doris. 'For goodness' sake think of something, Bobby.'

'I can't,' said Bobby, thinking hard. 'At least, I can't think of anything that Mam'zelle wouldn't know was a trick today. Oh – wait a minute though!'

The girls stared at Bobby expectantly. She turned to Janet. 'Where's that squeaking biscuit your brother sent you?' she asked.

Janet had a brother who was every bit as bad as Bobby and Janet where tricks were concerned. He had sent Janet a selection of jokes that week, and among them was a very realistic biscuit which, on being pressed between finger and thumb, squeaked loudly, rather like a cat. The girls had not thought that it was a very good trick.

'Rather babyish,' said Janet. 'Not a very good selection this time!'

But now Bobby had thought of some way to use the biscuit. Janet fished it out of her desk and gave it to her.

123

'Here you are,' she said. 'What are you going to do with it?'

Bobby pressed the biscuit slowly. It gave a pathetic squeaking sound. 'Doesn't it sound like a kitten?' she said with a grin. 'Now listen, everybody. The school cat has kittens, as you know. Well, when Mam'zelle comes into our classroom, she's going to find us talking about a lost kitten. We'll be very disturbed about it. And then, in the middle of the class, I press this biscuit – and Mam'zelle will think the lost kitten is somewhere in our room.'

Hilary chuckled. 'That's a good idea,' she said. 'And I know how we could improve on it too. I'll be outside in the passage, crawling about on my hands and knees, looking for the lost kitten, when Mam'zelle comes along to our room. I can tell her what I'm looking for.'

'Oooh, yes,' said Pat, looking thrilled. Hilary was very good at acting. 'Golly, we're going to have some fun!'

'Well, what happens in class *after* I've squeaked the biscuit will depend on all of you,' said Bobby. 'Look – there's Prudence coming. Don't tell her a word about it. You know what a sneak she is!'

The first form longed for the French lesson to come. They winked at one another whenever they thought of it. Miss Roberts caught one or two of the winks and pounced on the winkers.

'What is the joke, Hilary?' she asked coldly.

'There isn't a joke, Miss Roberts,' answered Hilary, opening her eyes wide as if astonished.

'Well, there had better *not* be,' said Miss Roberts.

'Go on with your geography map, please.'

Mam'zelle gave her French lesson after break. The girls went to their room quickly when break was over, giggling in delight. Prudence could not think why. Pam was not in the secret either, but she did not notice the chuckles of the girls. Pam was getting very much wrapped up in her own thoughts these days.

Hilary was left outside. The twins popped their heads out of the door and doubled themselves up with laughter when they saw Hilary on hands and knees, looking under a tall cupboard there, calling, 'Kitty, kitty, kitty!'

'Sh! Here comes Mam'zelle!' suddenly cried Pat to the class. She darted back to her seat, leaving Isabel to hold the door for Mam'zelle. Hilary was still outside, of course.

Mam'zelle came hurrying along on her big feet. Everyone always knew when Mam'zelle came, because she wore big, flat-heeled shoes like a man's, and made a loud clip-clap noise down the corridors.

Mam'zelle was most surprised to see Hilary crawling about outside the classroom. She stopped and stared.

'Hilary, *ma petite*! *Que faites-vous*?' she cried. 'What are you doing there? Have you lost something?'

'Kitty, kitty, kitty!' called Hilary. 'Mam'zelle, you haven't seen one of the school cat's kittens by any chance, have you? I'm looking and looking for the poor little lost thing.'

Mam'zelle looked up and down the passage. 'No, I have seen no little cat,' she said. 'Hilary, you must come to your class now. It is good of you to seek for the tiny cat, but it is not to be found.'

'Oh, Mam'zelle, just let me look a little longer,' begged Hilary. 'It might be in this cupboard. I thought I heard a sound.'

She opened the cupboard. The girls in the classroom, hearing the sound of conversation outside, wondered how Hilary was getting on. Isabel peeped out to see.

'Have you found the poor little kitten, Hilary?' she called. 'Oh, Mam'zelle, isn't it a shame? It will be so frightened.'

Mam'zelle marched into the classroom and put her books down on her desk. 'The little cat will be found somewhere,' she said. 'Go to your places. Hilary, for the last time I tell you to stop looking for the tiny cat and come to your French class.'

'Oh, Mam'zelle,' said Bobby, as Hilary came in and shut the door, 'do you think it has climbed up a chimney or something like that? I once knew a cat that got up our chimney at home, and arrived on the top of a chimney-pot!'

'And Mam'zelle, *we* had a kitten once that . . .' began Doris, quick to follow up and waste a few more minutes of the class. But Mam'zelle was not having any more fairy-tales about cats. She rapped on her desk, and Doris stopped her tale.

'*Assez*!' said Mam'zelle, beginning to frown. 'That is quite enough. Hilary, *will* you sit down? You surely do not imagine that the kitten is anywhere here?'

'Well, Mam'zelle, it *might* be,' said Hilary, looking all round. 'You know, my brother once had a cat that . . .'

'Any more tales about cats and the whole class will write me out two pages in French on the habits of the cat-family,' threatened Mam'zelle. At this threat everyone remained silent. Mam'zelle had a horrid way of carrying out her curious threats.

'Get out your grammar books,' said Mam'zelle. 'Open at page eighty-seven. Today we will devote the whole time to irregular verbs. Doris, you will begin.'

Doris gave a groan. She stood up to recite the verbs she had learnt. Poor Doris! No matter how much time she gave to her French preparation, every bit of it invariably went out of her head when she looked at Mam'zelle's expectant face. She began, in a halting voice.

'Doris, again you have not prepared your work properly,' said Mam'zelle, irritably. 'You will do it again. Pat, stand up. I hope you will give a better performance than Doris. You at least know how to roll your 'r's in the French way. R-r-r-r-r-r!'

The class giggled. Mam'zelle always sounded exactly as if she were growling like a dog when she rolled her r-r-r-r in her throat. Mam'zelle rapped on her desk.

'Silence! Pat, begin.'

But before Pat could begin, Bobby pressed the trick biscuit slowly and carefully between finger and thumb. A piteous squeak sounded somewhere in the room. Everyone looked up.

'The kitten!' said Pat, stopping her recital of verbs. 'The kitten!'

Even Mam'zelle listened. The squeak had been so very

much like a kitten in trouble. Bobby waited until Pat had begun her verbs again, and then she once more pressed the biscuit.

'EEEeeeeeeeee!' squeaked the biscuit, exactly like a cat. Pat stopped again and looked all round the room. Mam'zelle was puzzled.

'Where *is* the poor little creature?' said Kathleen. 'Oh, Mam'zelle – where can it be?'

'Mam'zelle, I'm pretty certain it must be up the chimney,' said Hilary, jumping up as if she was going to see.

'*Asseyez-vous*, Hilary!' rapped out Mam'zelle. 'You have looked enough for the little cat. Pat, continue.'

Pat began again, Bobby let her recite her verbs until she made a mistake – and then, before Mam'zelle could pounce on her mistake, Bobby pressed the biscuit once more.

A loud wail interrupted the recital of verbs. A babel of voices arose.

'Mam'zelle, the cat must be in the room!'

'Mam'zelle, do let's look for the poor little thing.'

'Mam'zelle, perhaps it's HURT!'

Bobby made the biscuit wail again. Mam'zelle rapped on her desk in despair.

'Sit still, please. I will see if the little cat is up the chimney.'

She left her desk and went to the fire-place. She bent down and tried to look up the chimney. Bobby pressed the biscuit softly and made a very small mew come. Mam'zelle half thought it came from up the chimney. She got a ruler and felt about there.

A shower of soot came down, and Mam'zelle jumped

back, her hand covered with soot. The class began to giggle.

'Mam'zelle, perhaps the cat's in the cupboard,' suggested Janet. 'Do let me look. I'm sure it's there.'

Mam'zelle was glad to leave the chimney. She gazed in dismay at her sooty hand.

'Hilary, open the cupboard,' she said at last. Hilary leapt to open it. Of course there was no animal there at all, but Hilary rummaged violently over the shelves, sending books and handwork material to the floor.

'Hilary! Is it necessary to do this?' cried Mam'zelle, beginning to lose her temper again. 'I begin to disbelieve in this cat. But I warn you, if it is a trick, I will punish you all with a terrible punishment. I go now to wash my hands. You will all learn the verbs on page eighty-eight while I am gone. You will not talk. You are bad children.'

Mam'zelle disappeared out of the room, holding her sooty hand before her. When the door shut, a gale of laughter burst out. Bobby squeaked the biscuit for all she was worth. Prudence stared in surprise at it. As no one had let her into the secret, she really had believed in the tale of the lost kitten. She looked at Bobby with a sour face. So Bobby had once more got away with a trick. How Prudence wished she could give her away to Mam'zelle!

'Well, wasn't that fine?' said Bobby, putting the biscuit into her pocket. 'Half the lesson gone, and hardly anyone has had to say their verbs. Good old biscuit! You can tell your brother it was a success, Janet!'

When Mam'zelle came back she was in one of her black tempers. She had felt sure, as she washed her hands, that there had been some trick about the lost kitten, but she could not for the life of her imagine what it was. She washed her hands grimly and stalked back to the first form, determined to get her own back somehow.

She chose Prudence to say her verbs next. Prudence stood up. She was bad at French, and she faltered over her verbs, trying in vain to get them right.

'Prrrrrudence! You are even more stupid than Dorrrris!' cried Mam'zelle, rolling her 'r's in her fiercest manner. 'Ah, this first form! You have learnt nothing this term! NOTHING, I say. Ahhhhhh! Tomorrow I will give you a test. A test to see what you have learnt. Prudence, do not stare at me like a duck that is dying! You and Doris are bad girls. You will not work for me. If you do not get more than half-marks tomorrow I shall go and complain to Miss Theobald. Ah, this first form!'

The girls listened in horror. A French test! Of all the things they hated, a French test was the worst. The girls always felt certain that Mam'zelle chose questions that hardly anyone could possibly answer!

Prudence sat down, hating Mam'zelle. She knew she would do badly in the test. She had cribbed most of her written work from Pam – but in a test she would have to rely on her own knowledge – unless she could copy Pam's answers.

The girl sat and brooded. If it hadn't been for Bobby's trick, Mam'zelle wouldn't have lost her temper and suggested a beastly, horrible test! How Prudence wished she could find some way to get out of it. If only she could – or better still, if only she could know what the test questions were to be, so that she might look up the answers first!

# 15

# Prudence is a cheat

The more Prudence thought about the French test, the angrier she felt with Bobby. I suppose she thinks those silly tricks of hers are clever! thought Prudence to herself. And now look what they've led to – a horrible French test that I know I shall fail hopelessly in. Then I shall get into a frightful row and perhaps be sent down to Miss Theobald!

She went to find Pam to talk to her about it. She felt sure Pam would be in the library, hunting for some learned book or other to read. On the way there she passed the open door of the mistresses' common-room. Prudence glanced in.

Mam'zelle was there alone. She was writing out what looked like a list of questions. Prudence felt certain they were the questions for the test. How she longed to have a look at them!

She stood at the door uncertainly, trying to think of some excuse to go in. Mam'zelle saw her shadow there and glanced up.

'Ah, Prudence!' she said, in rather a fierce voice. 'Ah! Tomorrow you will have this French test, yes? I will show you first formers what hard work really means!'

Prudence made up her mind quickly. She would go

into the common-room, and tell Mam'zelle about the trick – and perhaps she would be able to get a peep at the questions on Mam'zelle's desk! So in she went, looking the picture of wide-eyed innocence and goodness.

'Mam'zelle! I'm awfully sorry we played about so much in your class,' she began. 'It was all that silly trick, you know – the squeaking biscuit.'

Mam'zelle stared at Prudence as if the girl had suddenly gone mad.

'The squeaking biscuit?' said Mam'zelle, in the greatest astonishment. 'What is this nonsense you are saying?'

'Mam'zelle, it isn't nonsense,' said Prudence. 'You see, Bobby had a trick biscuit that squeaked like a cat when it was pressed . . .'

Prudence was doing her best to get a look at the French questions as she spoke. Apparently Mam'zelle had finished making them out. There were about twelve questions. Prudence managed to read the first one.

Mam'zelle listened to what Prudence was saying, and at once knew two things – the true explanation of the lost kitten – and that Prudence was what the English girls called 'sneaking'. Mam'zelle had been in England a long time and had learnt to regard sneaking with dislike, although when she had first arrived she had listened to tale-bearers and thought nothing of it. But through long years of being with English mistresses she had come to the conclusion that they were right about sneaks. On no account must they be encouraged.

So Mam'zelle's face suddenly changed, and became

hard and cold as Prudence went on speaking.

'And Bobby thought it would be a good idea if we wasted some of your lesson by pretending that a kitten was lost . . .' she went on. Then she stopped as she saw Mam'zelle's face.

'Prudence, you are a nasty little girl,' said Mam'zelle. 'Yes – a very nasty little girl. I do not like you. It may seem surprising to you – but I would rather have a silly trick played on me than listen to someone who sneaks about it! Go away at once. I do not like you at all.'

Prudence felt her face flame red. She was angry and hurt – and she hadn't been able to read more than one test question after all! Mam'zelle took up the paper and slipped it inside her desk, taking no more notice of Prudence. The girl went out of the room, ready to burst into angry tears.

'Well, I know *where* the questions are, anyway,' she thought, fiercely. 'I've a good mind to slip out of bed at night and have a look at them. Nobody would know. And I'd have a good chance of being top, then, and giving everyone a surprise! I'd love to see their faces if I got top marks!'

The more she thought about it, the more determined she became. 'I *will* get those questions somehow!' she decided. 'I don't care what happens – I will!'

She wondered if Mam'zelle would punish Bobby for the trick she had played, but to her surprise not a word was said about it that day, though Mam'zelle took prep and even had Bobby up to her desk to explain something to her.

I wonder she doesn't send Bobby to Miss Theobald, thought the girl, spitefully.

Mam'zelle's sense of humour had come to her rescue after Prudence had left the common-room that morning. She had felt angry with Bobby first of all – and then when she thought of herself poking up the chimney to find a kitten that wasn't there, she had begun to laugh. That was one very good thing about Mam'zelle – she really did have a sense of humour, and when she thought something was funny, she could laugh at it whole-heartedly and forget her annoyance. So her anger against the first formers melted away – though she was determined to give them the test, all the same.

She could not, however, resist giving Bobby a little shock. When the girl came up to her desk at prep Mam'zelle made a remark that caused Bobby to feel most uncomfortable.

'Do you like biscuits, Bobby?' she asked, her large brown eyes looking at Bobby through their lenses.

'Er – er – yes, Mam'zelle,' said Bobby, wondering what was coming next.

'I thought so,' said Mam'zelle, and then turned to Bobby's French book. Bobby did not dare to ask her what she meant, but she felt certain that Mam'zelle had found out about her trick. Who could have told her? Prudence, of course! Nasty little sneak! Bobby waited for Mam'zelle to say something more, and it was with great relief that she found Mam'zelle speaking about her French mistakes.

'Now you may go to your place,' said Mam'zelle. She gave Bobby a sharp look. 'You may like to know that I do not like biscuits as much as you do, *ma chère* Bobby!'

'No, Mam'zelle – er, I mean, yes, Mam'zelle,' said poor Bobby, and escaped to her seat as quickly as she could. If Mam'zelle *does* know what I did and isn't going to punish me, it's jolly decent of her, thought the girl. I'll work really hard in her classes if she's as decent as all that!

That night, when all the girls in her dormitory were asleep, Prudence sat up in bed. She listened to the steady breathing of the sleepers around her, and then slipped out of bed. It was very warm, and she did not put on her dressing-gown or slippers. She crept out of the room in her bare feet and went down the stairs to the mistresses' common-room. It was in complete darkness. Prudence had brought a torch with her, and she switched it on to see where Mam'zelle's desk was. Good – there it was, just in front of her.

Now I can just go all through the test questions, and look up the answers! thought Prudence, gleefully. It's lucky nobody woke up and saw me leaving the dormitory.

But somebody *had* seen her leaving the dormitory!

That somebody was Carlotta, who always slept very lightly indeed, waking at the least sound. She had heard the click of the door being opened, and had sat up at once. She dimly saw a figure vanishing through the doorway, and wondered who it was. Perhaps it was someone from the next dormitory. She decided to go and see. Sometimes a girl from another dormitory was dared to slip into someone else's room at night and play some kind of joke.

Carlotta slipped out of bed. She went to the dormitory

where Bobby, Pam, Doris, and others slept. She popped her head inside. All was quiet – but one girl was awake. It was Bobby. She saw the door opening, and the dim light from the passage came into the room, showing up the figure at the door.

'Who's there?' whispered Bobby.

'Me,' said Carlotta. 'I saw somebody slipping out of our dormitory and I thought it might be someone from yours, playing a joke.'

'Well, we're all here,' said Bobby, looking down the line of beds. 'Are you sure it wasn't somebody out of your *own* room?'

'Never thought of that,' whispered back Carlotta. 'I'll go and see.' She went and found that Prudence's bed was empty. She slipped back again to Bobby and went to her bed.

'Prudence is gone,' she whispered. 'What do you think she's doing? I bet she's up to some mischief, don't you?'

'Well, let's go and see,' said Bobby, and slid quietly out of bed. Together the two made their way down the passage, and then down the stairs. They stood and listened at the bottom, wondering where Prudence was.

'There's a light coming from the mistresses' common-room,' whispered Carlotta. 'Perhaps she is in there. What *can* she be doing?'

'I'm not sure I quite like spying like this,' said Bobby, a little uncomfortably. But Carlotta had no doubts of that sort. She went quietly on bare feet to the half open door of the common-room. She looked in – and there she saw

Prudence carefully reading the list of French test questions, a French grammar book beside her. She was looking up the answers one by one.

Both girls knew at once what she was doing. Bobby had very strict ideas of honour and she was really horrified and shocked. Carlotta was not shocked, because she had seen many odd things in her life – also she knew Prudence well and was not at all surprised to find her cheating in such an outrageous way.

Bobby went into the room at once, and Prudence was so startled that she dropped the grammar book on the floor. She stared at Bobby and Carlotta with horror.

'What are you doing?' said Bobby, so angry that she forgot to whisper. 'Cheating?'

'No, I'm not,' said Prudence, making up her mind to brazen it out. 'I just came to look something up in the French grammar book, ready for the test tomorrow. So there!'

Carlotta darted to the desk and picked up the list of questions. 'See, Bobby,' she cried. 'She *is* cheating! Here are the test questions.'

Bobby looked at Prudence with the utmost scorn. 'What a hypocrite you are, Prudence!' she said. 'You go about pretending to be so good and religious and proper – and yet you sneak and cheat whenever you get a chance. You look down on Carlotta because she was a circus girl – but I tell you, *we* look down on *you* because you are all the things people hate worse than any other in school, or in life – you are cunning, deceitful, untruthful – and an out-and-out cheat!'

These were terrible things to hear. Prudence burst out sobbing, and put her head down on the desk. A pile of books upset and fell with thuds to the floor. Nobody noticed the noise they made, for all three girls were too wrapped up in what was happening.

It so happened that Miss Theobald's bedroom was just below the mistresses' common-room. She heard the succession of thuds and wondered what the noise could be. She thought she heard the sound of voices too. She switched on her light and looked at her watch. It was a quarter-past two! Whoever could be up at that time of night?

Miss Theobald put on her dressing-gown, tied the belt firmly round her waist, put on her slippers, and left the room. She went upstairs to the corridor that led to the mistresses' common-room. She arrived at the door just in time to hear the end of Bobby's scornful speech. She paused in the greatest astonishment. Whatever could be happening?

# 16

# Miss Theobald deals with three girls

'Girls,' said Miss Theobald, in her clear low voice. 'Girls! What are you doing here?'

There was a petrified silence as all three girls saw the head mistress standing at the door. A cold chill came over Prudence's heart, and Bobby had the shock of her life. Only Carlotta seemed undisturbed.

'Well?' said Miss Theobald, going into the room, and shutting the door. 'I really think some explanation of this scene is needed. Roberta, surely you can explain?'

'Yes, I can,' blurted out Bobby. 'Surely you can guess what Carlotta and I discovered Prudence doing, Miss Theobald?'

'She is cheating,' said Carlotta, in her little foreign-sounding voice. 'She is looking at the French test questions and finding the answers, Miss Theobald, so that she will be top tomorrow. But it is nothing surprising. Prudence is like that.'

Prudence broke out into loud sobbing again.

'I wasn't, I wasn't,' she wailed. 'Carlotta only says that because I found out she was nothing but a circus girl. I hate her! I hate Bobby too – but Carlotta is the worst of the lot, always showing off and bragging about her circus life.'

Carlotta laughed. 'I am glad you hate me, Prudence,' she said. 'I would not care to be liked by you! You are worse than anyone I have ever met in circus camps. Much worse!'

'Be quiet, Carlotta,' said Miss Theobald. She was very worried. This was a dreadful thing to happen. 'Go back to bed, all of you. I will deal with this in the morning. Is Prudence in the same dormitory as you two?'

'No, she's in mine, but not in Bobby's,' said Carlotta.

'Well – go back, all of you,' said Miss Theobald. 'If I hear another sound tonight, I shall treat the matter even more seriously tomorrow.'

She watched the three girls go back to their dormitories, and then went to her own room, wondering how to deal with things in the best way. Had she done right in letting Carlotta, the little circus girl, come to St Clare's? She might have known that the secret wouldn't be kept! And now there was Prudence Arnold to deal with – Miss Theobald could not like the girl any more than anyone else did. And Roberta – what should she say to her? She had had bad reports of her work from everyone!

The three girls went back to their beds. Carlotta fell asleep again at once. She rarely worried about anything and she did not feel any cause to be upset. Bobby lay and thought for a long time. She disliked and despised Prudence – but she did not want the girl to get into serious trouble because of her.

Prudence was the most upset of the three. It was a very serious matter to be caught cheating. She had always set herself up to be such a model – so honest and straight and had always condemned underhand, mean, or silly tricks. Now everyone would know she was not what she seemed. And it was all because of that hateful interfering Bobby and Carlotta. She felt a great surge of bitterness against Carlotta, who had so calmly told Miss Theobald what the two girls had found her doing. Prudence did not realize that practically every girl had seen through her silly pretences and had set her down as a smug hypocrite and sneak.

Next day the three girls were called into Miss Theobald's room one by one. First Carlotta, who told Miss Theobald again, quite calmly and straightforwardly, what they had found Prudence doing, and also added a few remarks of her own about Prudence.

'She looks down on me because I was a circus girl,' said Carlotta, 'but Miss Theobald, no circus would keep a person like Prudence for more than a week. I think she is a dangerous girl.'

Miss Theobald said nothing to this but in her heart she agreed with Carlotta. Prudence was dangerous. She would do no good to St Clare's, and privately Miss Theobald doubted if St Clare's would do much good for Prudence. She prided herself on the knowledge that it was very few girls indeed that St Clare's would not benefit – but it seemed to her as if Prudence was one of those few. She was the only child of doting, indulging parents, who believed that Prudence was all she seemed. Poor Prudence! What a pity her father and mother hadn't been sensible with her, and punished her when she did wrong, instead of getting upset and begging her to do better!

Miss Theobald had Bobby in next. Bobby did not want to say much about Prudence, and she was surprised to find that Miss Theobald looked at her coldly, and did not give her even a small smile when she came in.

'It is an unpleasant thing to find anyone in the act of cheating,' said Miss Theobald, looking straight at Bobby. 'I expect you hate the idea of cheating almost worse than anything else, Roberta.'

'Yes, Miss Theobald,' said Bobby, who was an honest and truthful girl, in spite of all the tricks she played. 'I think cheating is horrible. I'd just hate myself if I cheated like Prudence.'

Then Miss Theobald said a surprising thing. 'It is odd to me, Roberta,' she said, 'that you, who seem to have such strict ideas about cheating, should be such a cheat yourself.'

Bobby stared at Miss Theobald as if she couldn't believe her ears. 'What did you say, Miss Theobald?' she asked at last. 'I think I didn't hear it correctly.'

'Yes, you did, Roberta,' said Miss Theobald. 'I said that it was odd that *you* should be a cheat, when you hold such strict ideas about cheating.'

'I'm not a cheat,' said Bobby, her cheeks crimson, and her eyes beginning to sparkle with anger and surprise. 'I've never cheated in my life.'

'I don't know about *all* your life,' said the head mistress, 'but I do know about the last two months of it, Roberta. Why have your parents sent you here? To have a good time and nothing but a good time? Why are they paying high fees for you? In order to let you slack and play tricks the whole time? You *are* cheating, Roberta – yes, cheating badly. You are cheating your parents, who are willing to pay for you to learn what we can teach you here – and you won't learn. You are cheating the school, for you have good brains and could do well for St Clare's – but you won't try. And last of all you are cheating yourself – depriving yourself of all the benefits that hard work, well done, can bring you, and you are weakening your character instead of making it strong and fine, because you will not accept duty and responsibility. You just want to go your own way, do as little work as you can, and make yourself popular by being amusing and thinking out ingenious jokes and tricks to entertain your form. I think, in your own way, you are just as much a cheat as Prudence is.'

Bobby's face went white. No one had ever said anything like this to her before. She had always been popular with girls and teachers alike – but here was the head mistress pointing out cold and horrid truths that Bobby had never even thought of before. It was dreadful.

The girl sat quite still and said nothing at all. 'You had better go now, Roberta,' said Miss Theobald. 'I would like you to think over what I have said and see if your sense of honesty is as high as you think it to be – if it is, you will admit to yourself that I am right, and perhaps I shall then get good reports of you.'

Bobby stood up, still white. She mumbled something to Miss Theobald and went out of the room as if she was in a dream. She had had a real shock. It had never before occurred to Bobby that it was possible to cheat in many more ways than the ordinary one.

Prudence was the last of the three called before the head mistress. She was likely to be the most difficult to deal with. Miss Theobald decided that plain speaking was the best. Prudence must know exactly how she stood – and make her own choice.

The girl came in, looking rather frightened. She tried to look Miss Theobald straight in the eyes but could not. The head told her to sit down, and then looked just as coldly at her as she had looked at Bobby.

'Please, Miss Theobald,' began Prudence, who always believed in getting a word in first, 'please don't think the worst of me.'

'Well, I *do* think the worst of you,' said the head mistress at once. 'The very worst. And unfortunately I know it to be true. Prudence, I know the character of every girl in this school. It is my business to know it. I may not know what type of brain you have, I may not know exactly where you stand in class, or what your gifts and capabilities are, without referring to your form mistress – but at any rate I know your characters – the good and bad in you, the possibilities in your nature, your tendencies, your faults, your virtues. These I know very well. And therefore I know all too clearly, Prudence, what you really are.'

Prudence burst into tears. She often found this useful when people were what she called 'being unkind' to her. The tears had no effect at all on Miss Theobald. She stared at Prudence all the more coldly.

'Cry if you wish,' she said, 'but I would think more of you if you faced up to me and listened with a little courage. I need not tell you what you are, Prudence. I need not show you the dishonesty, deceitfulness and spite in your own nature. You are clever enough to know them yourself – and alas, cunning enough to use them, and to hide them too. St Clare's, Prudence, has nothing to offer a girl like you – unless you have enough courage to face up to yourself, and try to tear out the unpleasant failings that are spoiling and weakening what character you have. I do not want to keep you at St Clare's unless you can do this. Think it over and face things out honestly with yourself. I give you to the end of the term to make up your mind. Otherwise, Prudence, I will not keep you here.'

This was actually the only kind of treatment that Prudence really understood. She stared in horror at Miss Theobald.

'But – but – what would my father and mother say?' she half-whispered.

'That rests with you,' said the head. 'Now go, please. I am busy this morning, and have already wasted too much time on you and the others.'

Prudence went out of the room, as shocked and horrified as poor Bobby had been a few minutes earlier. She had to get her books and go to her form for a lesson, but she heard practically nothing of what Miss Lewis, the history teacher, was saying. Bobby heard very little too. Both girls were busy with their own thoughts.

After school that morning, Bobby disappeared. Pat and Isabel saw her running off in the direction of the tennis-court.

'Doesn't she look white?' said Pat. 'I wonder if anything's up?'

'Let's go and see,' said Isabel. So they went to find Bobby. She was nowhere on the courts – but Pat caught sight of a white blouse and navy skirt in a little copse of trees by the courts. She ran up to see if Bobby was there.

'Bobby, what's up?' she cried, for it was quite plain to see that Bobby was in trouble. Her usually merry face, with its sparkling eyes, was white and drawn.

'Go away, please,' said Bobby, in a tight sort of voice. 'I want to think. I – I – I've been accused of cheating – and – I've got to think about it.'

'*You*! You, accused of cheating!' cried Pat, in angry amazement. 'What rot! Who dared to do that? You tell me, and I'll go and tell them what I think of them.'

'It was Miss Theobald,' said Bobby, lifting her troubled face and looking at the twins.

'Miss *Theobald*!' said the twins, in the greatest astonishment. 'But why? How awful of her! We'll go and tell her she's wrong.'

'Well – she's not wrong,' said Bobby. 'I see she's right. She said I was a cheat because I let my parents pay high fees for me to learn what St Clare's could teach – and I wasted my time and wouldn't work – and that was cheating, because I've got good brains. She said I was cheating my parents – and the school – and myself too. It was – simply awful.'

The twins stared uncomfortably at Bobby. They couldn't think of a word to say. Bobby motioned to them to go away.

'Go away, please,' she said. 'I've got to think this out. I simply must. It's – it's somehow very important. I do play the fool a lot – but I'm not such an idiot as not to see that I've come to a sort of – sort of – cross-roads in my life. I've got to choose which way I'll go. And I've got to choose by myself. So leave me alone for a bit, will you?'

'Of course, Bobby,' said Pat, understanding. She and Isabel ran off, admiring Bobby for her ability to face herself, and make up her own mind what she was going to do.

And there was no doubt as to what Bobby was going to do. Her tremendous sense of honesty and fairness made her see at once that Miss Theobald was perfectly right. She had been given good brains, and she was wasting them. That was cheating. She had good parents who wanted her to go to a fine school and learn from good teachers. She was cheating them too. And perhaps worst of all she was cheating herself, and growing into a weaker and poorer character than she needed to be – and the world wanted fine, strong characters, able to help others on – not poor, weak, don't-care people who themselves needed to be helped all the time.

I badly want to be the sort of person who can lead others, and guide them, thought Bobby, pulling at the grass, as she sat thinking. I want others to lean on me – not me on them. Well – I've had my fun. Now I'll work. I'll just show Miss Roberts what I really can do when I make up my mind. I've already shown Belinda and Miss Wilton what I can do at sports when I try. I'll go straight to Miss Theobald and tell her now. I – I don't feel as if I like her very much now – she had such cold, angry eyes when she looked at me. But I'd better go and tell her – I'll get it off my chest and make a fresh start.

Poor Bobby felt nervous as she ran back to the school. Miss Theobald had given her a real shock, and she dreaded seeing her again, and felt half frightened as she thought of looking into the head mistress's scornful eyes. But Bobby had courage, and she was soon knocking at Miss Theobald's door.

'Come in,' said a calm voice, and Bobby went in. She went straight to the head mistress's desk.

'Miss Theobald,' she said, 'I've come to say I know you were right. I *have* been cheating – and I didn't realize it. But – I'm not going to cheat any more. Please believe me. I really do mean what I say, and you can trust me to – to do my very best from today.'

Bobby said this bravely, looking straight at Miss Theobald as she spoke. Her voice trembled a little, but she said her little speech right to the end.

Miss Theobald smiled her rare, sweet smile, and her eyes became warm and admiring. 'My dear child,' she said, and her voice was warm too, 'my dear child, I knew quite well that you would make this decision, and that you would soon come to tell me. I am proud of you – and I am going to be even more proud of you in the future. You are honest enough by nature to be able to see and judge your own self clearly – and that is a great thing. Never lose that honesty, Bobby – always be honest with yourself, know your own motives for what they are, good or bad, make your own decisions firmly and justly – and you will be a fine, strong character, of some real use in this muddled world of ours!'

'I'll try, Miss Theobald,' said Bobby, happily, so glad to see the warmth and friendliness in the head's face that she felt she could work twelve hours a day if necessary! How could she have thought she didn't like Miss Theobald? How *could* she?

She's one of the finest people I've ever met, thought the girl, as she left the room with a light step. No wonder she's head of a great school like St Clare's! We are jolly lucky to have her.

Miss Theobald was happy too. Bobby had pleased her beyond measure. It was good to feel that she had been successful in handling an obstinate character like Bobby's – now she might hope that the girl would have a splendid influence on the others, instead of the opposite.

If I could only hope that Prudence would have the

same kind of courage as Bobby! thought the head. But Prudence, I'm afraid, is not brave enough to face up to herself. That's her only chance – but I don't believe she will take it!

# 17

# Sadie gets a letter

Whilst Bobby was thinking out things for herself, and making her big decision, Prudence was also brooding over all that Miss Theobald had said. Mixed up with her brooding was a hatred of Carlotta, who seemed to be at the bottom of Prudence's troubles. Prudence could not see that it was her own jealousy of the girl that caused her troubles, filling her with ideas of spite and revenge. No one can ever see things clearly when jealousy or envy cast a fog over the mind.

Prudence felt that she had to get right with Miss Theobald. The girl could never bear to feel that anyone was despising her. But she had not got Bobby's courage – she dared not face the head again. Also, in her heart of hearts she was afraid that Miss Theobald would see that her repentance was not real – that it was only to make things more comfortable!

So Prudence wrote a note, and slipped it on Miss Theobald's desk, when she knew she was not in her room. The head found it there and opened it. She read it and sighed. She did not believe one word of the letter.

*Dear Miss Theobald,*

*I have thought over what you said to me, and I do assure you I am sorry and ashamed, and I will do my best in future to turn over a new leaf and have a good influence on others.*

Little humbug! thought Miss Theobald, sadly. I suppose she really believes she *is* going to turn over a new leaf. Well – we shall see!

Pat and Isabel were glad to see that Bobby looked happier that evening. She smiled at them, and her old merry twinkle came back.

'I'm all right again,' she said. 'But from now on I'm going to play fair – I'm going to use my brains and work. No more squeaking biscuits for *me*!'

The twins and Janet looked sorry. 'Oh,' said Pat in disappointment, 'Bobby – you don't mean to say you're going to go all prim and proper like that awful Prudence – never make another joke or play another trick?'

'Golly!' said Janet. 'I couldn't bear that, Bobby. For pity's sake, tell us you're going to be the same jolly old Bobby – the Don't-Care Bobby we all like so much!'

Bobby laughed and slipped her arm through Janet's. 'Don't worry,' she said. 'I *am* going to play the game now and work hard – but I shan't go all prim and proper. I couldn't. I shall be playing tricks all right – but I don't particularly want to be Don't-Care Bobby any more. I *do* care now, you see!'

Bobby kept her word to Miss Theobald, of course. She worked hard and steadily in class, and was surprised to find how well her mind worked when she really set it to something – and she was even more surprised to find how enjoyable good work was!

'I should never be able to slave at my lessons like you do though, Pam,' she said, looking at the thirteen-year-old girl hunched over a book. 'You're looking awfully pale lately. I'm sure you read too much.'

Pam *was* pale – and not only pale but unhappy-looking too. She was terribly sorry now that she had made firm friends with Prudence, because she was beginning to dislike her heartily, but was not strong enough to tell her so. So she found refuge in her lessons, and was working twice as hard as anyone else. She smiled a pale smile at Bobby, and envied her. Bobby didn't mind saying anything that came into her mind, and was as strong as Pam was weak. How Pam wished she could have made friends with Bobby instead of with Prudence!

Prudence was feeling rather pleased with herself. Miss Theobald had not said anything about her letter and the girl felt sure it had made a good impression on the head. For some reason Mam'zelle had not given the French test after all, so the class had heaved a sigh of relief – especially Prudence, who felt certain that Carlotta would blurt out that she, Prudence, had seen the questions before.

Things are going better, thought Prudence. If only that beastly Carlotta could get into a row! She just flaunts about as if she were a princess and not a common little circus girl! I wonder if she visits any of her low-down friends any more? I saw her going off early yesterday morning before breakfast.

It was true that Carlotta did go off each morning – but not to visit any circus friend. She had discovered that some lovely hunting horses were kept in a field not far off, and the girl was visiting them regularly. Sometimes she rode one or other bareback, if there was nobody about. The girl was quite mad about horses, and never lost a chance of going near them if she could.

Nobody knew this. Prudence knew Carlotta was slipping off, but told no one else, for she had found that none of the girls encouraged her confidences at all. She determined to keep a watch herself.

She and Pam went off one afternoon together, Pam not at all pleased about it, but not daring to say no. Prudence had seen Carlotta going off – but somehow or other she missed following her, and the two girls stopped in a little lane, whilst Prudence tried to think where Carlotta had gone.

A man came riding by on a bicycle. He was not a pleasant-looking fellow and his eyes were set very close together. He got off his bicycle when he came up to the girls, and spoke to them. His voice sounded rather foreign, and had a slow American drawl with it. Prudence felt absolutely certain that he had come to see Carlotta.

'Excuse me,' said the man. 'Am I anywhere near St Clare's school?'

'Well – about a mile away,' said Prudence. 'Why? Do you want to see someone there?'

'I should like to,' said the man. 'It's very important

indeed. I suppose you couldn't take a message for me?'

Prudence's heart beat fast. What trouble she could get Carlotta into now! What would Miss Theobald say if she knew Carlotta was slipping out to see awful people like this?

'Of course I could take a message for you,' she said.

The man took a letter from his pocket and handed it to Prudence. 'Don't you tell a single soul,' he said. 'It's very very important. I'll be here at eleven o'clock tonight without fail.'

'All right,' said Prudence. 'I'll see to it for you.'

'You're a brick,' said the man. 'You're dandy! I'll give you a fine present, see if I don't!'

Someone else came down the lane at that moment, and the man jumped on his bicycle and rode away, saluting the two girls as he went. Pam shivered a little.

'Prudence! I don't like him! I don't think you ought to have spoken to him. You know it's a rule we never speak to strangers. You're not going to get Carlotta into trouble are you?'

'Oh, be quiet!' said Prudence, impatiently. She pushed the letter into her pocket without looking at it. 'Aren't I *doing* something for Carlotta, silly? Aren't I taking a message to her from a friend? What awful friends she has, too!'

Pam was worried. Her head ached, and she felt miserable. She wished she had never, never become friendly with Prudence. Her mind turned once again to her work – she could only forget things if she worked. She hadn't been sleeping well at night, and her work was becoming difficult to do which made her worry all the more.

'Now listen to me, Pam,' said Prudence. 'You and I are going to go out tonight at half-past ten and come here. We are going to hide behind the hedge, and hear what goes on between our dear Carlotta and her circus friend. If she is planning any more escapades, we can report them.'

Pam stared at her friend in distress. 'I can't do that,' she said. 'I can't.'

'You've got to,' said Prudence, and she stared at Pam out of her pale blue eyes. Pam felt too tired and weak to argue. She simply nodded her head miserably and turned back to go home. The girls walked back in silence, Prudence thinking with delight that now she had Carlotta at her mercy!

As soon as they got back to school Hilary hailed Prudence. 'Prudence! You know quite well it's your turn to brush up all the tennis-balls and get them clean this week. You haven't done it once, you lazy creature. You jolly well do it now, or you'll be sorry.'

'I've just got to take a message to somebody,' said Prudence. 'I won't be a minute.'

'You just let somebody else take the message,' said Hilary, annoyed. 'I know your little ways, Prudence – you'll *just* do this and you'll *just* do that – and the little jobs you ought to do aren't done!'

'*I'll* take the letter, Prudence,' said Pam, wearily. She felt that she could not stand arguments a minute more. Prudence handed her the letter with a sulky face. Pam went off to find Carlotta. She was in the common-room with the others. Pam went up to her and gave her the letter.

'This is for you,' she said. Carlotta took the note, and, without looking at the envelope, tore it open. She read the first line or two in evident amazement. Then she looked at the envelope.

'Why, it isn't for me,' she said, looking round for Pam, who, however, had gone. 'It's for Sadie. I suppose Pam didn't see her name on the envelope. How odd! Where's Sadie, Alison?'

'Doing her hair,' said Alison. There was a shout of laughter at this. When Sadie was missed she was always either Doing Her Hair, Doing Her Nails or Doing Her Face. Carlotta grinned and went to find her.

'Hi, Sadie,' she said, 'here's a note for you. Sorry I opened it by mistake, but that little idiot of a Pam gave it to me instead of you. I haven't read it.'

'Who's it from? How did Pam get it?' asked Sadie curiously, taking the note.

'Don't know,' said Carlotta, and went. Sadie opened the envelope and took out the letter inside. She read it and her face changed. She sat down on the bed, and thought hard. She read the letter again.

*Dear Miss Sadie,*
*Do you remember your old nanny, Hannah? Well, I'm over here and I'd like to see you. I don't like to come to the school. Can you come down to the lane by the farm and see me for a*

*few minutes? I'll be there at eleven o'clock tonight.*

*Hannah*


Sadie had been very fond of Hannah, who had been her nanny and her mother's help for some years. She was astonished that Hannah should be in England, for she had thought she was in America. Why did she want to see her? Had anything happened? Sadie wondered whether to tell Alison or not – and then she decided not to. Alison was a nice girl and a pretty one, but she was a feather-head. She might go and bleat it out to somebody!

Sadie tucked the note into her pocket and went downstairs. 'Hallo!' said Alison. 'I was wondering whenever you were coming down. It's nearly supper-time.'

Sadie was rather silent at supper-time. She felt puzzled and a little worried. She thought she would ask Pam where she had got the note from – but Pam was not at supper.

'She's got a frightful headache and Miss Roberts sent her to Matron,' said Janet. 'She's got a temperature.'

Prudence was quite pleased to think she would not have Pam with her that night after all. She was getting a little tired of pretending to Pam that everything she was doing was for Carlotta's good. She looked at Carlotta to see if the girl showed any signs of receiving the letter. Carlotta saw her glancing her way and made one of her peculiarly rude faces. Prudence looked down her nose in disgust and turned away. Carlotta grinned. She didn't care a ha'-penny for Prudence and delighted in shocking her.

# 18

# An exciting night

That evening Sadie lay awake until the clock struck a quarter to eleven. It was still fairly light, but everyone in the dormitory was asleep. Sadie got up quietly and dressed. No one heard her. She slipped out of the dormitory and down the stairs. In a few moments she was out of the garden-door and in the school grounds. Behind her slipped a dark little shadow – Prudence! Prudence thought that she was following Carlotta, of course. She had no idea it was Sadie. Prudence had got up at a quarter-past ten, and had slipped out of the dormitory next to Sadie's, afraid that if she waited any later, Carlotta might get away before she had a chance of keeping up with her. She had felt so certain that it was Carlotta the letter had been for – she had never even looked at the envelope to see what name was written there!

Now, at about a quarter-past eleven, Alison awoke suddenly with a sore throat. She cleared it and swallowed. It felt most unpleasant. She knew that Sadie had some lozenges and she decided to wake her and ask for them. So the girl slipped out of bed and went to Sadie's cubicle.

She put out her hand to shake Sadie – and to her great astonishment found that she was not there! Her bed was empty! Her clothes had gone – so she had dressed. Alison sat down on the bed in surprise. She was hurt. Why hadn't Sadie told her she was going somewhere? But where in the world could she have gone? There couldn't be a midnight feast or anything like that – because it was obvious that everyone was in bed – unless the other dormitory was holding a feast and had asked Sadie.

Well, Sadie might at least have told me, even if *I* wasn't asked, thought Alison, aggrieved. I'll go and peep in at the twins' dormitory and see if there's anything going on there.

So she slipped into the next dormitory – but everyone's bed seemed filled – with the exception of one. How odd. Alison stood thinking – and then she heard a whisper. It was Pat.

'Who's that? What are you doing?'

'Oh, Pat – are you awake?' said Alison in a low voice, going to Pat's bed. 'I say – Sadie's gone. She's dressed – and her bed is empty. I don't know why, Pat, but I feel worried about it. Sadie didn't seem herself this evening – she was all quiet and sort of worried. I noticed it.'

Pat sat up. She was puzzled. Sadie didn't usually do anything out of the ordinary at all. 'Wherever can she have gone?' she said.

'There's one bed empty in your dorm, too,' said Alison. 'Whose is it?'

'Golly – it's Prudence's,' said Pat, in astonishment. 'Don't tell me those two are somewhere together! I thought Sadie detested Prudence.'

'She does,' said Alison, more puzzled than ever. A movement in the next bed made them look round. Carlotta's voice came to them, low and guarded.

'What *are* you two doing? You'll wake everyone up! Anything up?'

'Carlotta – it's so funny – both Sadie and Prudence are gone from their beds,' said Pat. Carlotta sat up at once. She remembered the note she had given to Sadie.

'I wonder if it's anything to do with the note that Pam gave to me instead of to Sadie,' she said.

'What note?' asked Alison. Carlotta told her, and Pat and Alison listened in surprise.

'Somehow I think there's something a bit odd about this,' said Carlotta. 'I do really.'

'So do I,' said Alison, uncomfortably. 'I'm awfully fond of Sadie. You don't think – you don't think, do you – that's she being kidnapped – or anything. She said once that she nearly had been, over in America. She's awfully rich, you know. Her mother sent her over here because she was afraid she might be kidnapped again in America. She told me that.'

Carlotta could more readily believe this than the more stolid Pat. She got out of bed.

'I think the first thing we'd better do is to ask Pam where she got that note,' said Carlotta.

'She's in the sickbay,' said Pat.

'Well, we'll go there then,' said Carlotta. 'Let's wake Isabel. Hurry!'

It was not long before the twins, Alison and Carlotta

were creeping across the school grounds to the sickbay. This was where any girl who was ill was kept in bed. The door was locked, but a downstairs window was open. Carlotta got in quietly. She could climb like a cat!

'Stay here,' she whispered to the others. 'We don't want to wake Matron. I'll find Pam and ask her what we want to know.'

She made her way through the dark little room and up the stairs to where a dim light was burning in a bedroom. Here Pam lay, wide awake, trying to cool her burning forehead with a wet handkerchief. She was amazed and frightened when she saw Carlotta creeping into the room.

'Sh!' whispered Carlotta. 'It's only me, Carlotta! Pam – where did you get that note from – the one you gave me?'

'Prudence and I met a funny-looking man down the lane by the farm this afternoon,' said Pam. 'He said he wanted to send a message to someone. So Prudence took the note and meant to give it to you. But I had to give it to you instead. The man wanted you to meet him there at eleven o'clock tonight – or to meet somebody there. Why? What's happened?'

'The note wasn't for me – it was for Sadie,' said Carlotta, feeling puzzled. 'Did the man *say* it was for me?'

'Well, now I come to think of it, no names were mentioned at all,' said Pam, frowning as she tried to remember the conversation. 'But somehow Prudence seemed to think we were talking about you.'

'She would!' said Carlotta, grimly. 'I know where she is too! She thought that the man was one of my low-down circus friends, as she calls them – and she wanted to get me down there – and she would spy on me and report me. I know Prudence! But as it happens, the note *wasn't* for me – and I've a feeling that there's some dirty work going on round poor Sadie. She's gone down to the lane by the farm – and I bet Prudence has gone there too – to spy.'

'Yes, she has,' said Pam, feeling frightened and miserable. Tears ran down her cheeks. 'Oh, Carlotta – I'm supposed to be Prudence's friend – but I do so dislike her. It's making me ill. I'm really afraid of her.'

'Don't you worry,' said Carlotta, comfortingly, and she patted Pam's hot hand. 'We'll deal with Miss Sour-Milk Prudence after this. She'll get herself into serious trouble if she's not careful.'

The girl slipped away and went back to the others, who were waiting impatiently by the open window. She told them in a few words all she had learnt.

'Had we better wake Miss Theobald?' said Pat, troubled.

'No – we'll see what's happening first. It mayn't be anything much,' said Carlotta. 'Come on down to the lane by the farm.'

The four girls took bicycles and cycled away in the dark. The summer twilight was just enough for them to see their way. Half-way to the farm they met a sobbing figure running up towards them. It was Prudence!

'Prudence! What's the matter? What's happening?' cried Pat in alarm.

'Oh, Pat! Is it you? Oh, Pat! Something dreadful has happened!' sobbed Prudence. 'Sadie has been kidnapped!

She has, she has! I thought I was following Carlotta when I went out this evening just before eleven – but it was Sadie after all – and when she got near the farm, two men came up and took hold of her. And they dragged her to a hidden car and put her in. I was hiding behind the hedge.'

'Did you hear them say anything?' demanded Carlotta.

'Yes – they said something about a place called Jalebury,' wept Prudence. 'Where is it?'

'Jalebury!' said Carlotta, in astonishment. 'I know where Jalebury is. Why, that's where the circus camp went to! Are you sure you heard them say they were taking Sadie there, Prudence?'

Prudence was quite sure. Carlotta jumped on her bicycle. 'I'm just going to cycle to the telephone kiosk down the lane,' she called. 'The kidnappers will get a shock when they get to Jalebury!'

She rode to the kiosk, jumped off her bicycle, disappeared into the little telephone box, and looked up a number there. In a minute or two her excited voice fill·d the kiosk as she poured out her story to someone, and asked for their help.

In about five minutes she was back with the others. 'I telephoned the circus camp,' she said. 'They'll be on the watch for the car. They'll stop it and surround it – and if they don't rescue Sadie, I'll eat my hat!'

'Oh, Carlotta – you really are marvellous!' said Pat. 'But wouldn't it have been better to call the police?'

'I never thought of that,' said Carlotta. 'You see – in circus life we don't somehow call in the police. Now – I'm off to join in the fun! I know my way to Jalebury. But I'm not going by bike!'

'How are you going then?' asked Pat.

'On horseback!' said Carlotta. 'I shall borrow one of the hunters I've ridden on in the early morning. They are quite near here – and any of them will come to me if I call to them. I'm going to be in at the fun!'

The girl disappeared into a field. The twins, Alison, and Prudence stared after her in the starlight. Carlotta was such a surprising person. She went straight for what she wanted, and nothing could stop her. In a few minutes they heard the sound of galloping hoofs – and that was the last they saw of Carlotta that night!

# 19

## Carlotta to the rescue!

Carlotta knew the countryside around very well. She took the horse across fields and hills, her sense of direction telling her exactly where to go. She thought hard all the time, and smiled grimly when Prudence came into her mind.

'She's gone just too far this time!' she thought, as she galloped on through the night, the horse responding marvellously to the girl's sure hands. 'I do hope I get to Jalebury in time to see the fun.'

She didn't get there in time! But when she reached the little town after some time, she saw lights in the big field where the camp was, and galloped swiftly to it. She put the horse to jump the fence that ran round the field and it rose high in the air.

A voice hailed her. 'Who's that?'

'Oh, Jim – it's me, Carlotta!' she cried. 'Has anything happened? Did you get my message?'

'We did,' said the man, coming up to take the panting horse. 'And we've got the girl for you. Mighty pretty, isn't she?'

'Very,' said Carlotta, with a laugh. 'And if I know anything about Sadie, she wanted to borrow a comb and do her hair, or powder her nose, as soon as you rescued her! Tell me what happened.'

'Well, as soon as we got your message we dragged a caravan out of the field and set it across the road there – see, where it runs down into the town,' said the man, pointing in the starlight to where a road, not much wider than a big lane, ran between high hedges. 'Nobody was about, and not a car came by – till suddenly one appeared, racing along. We guessed it must be the one we wanted.'

'Oh – if only I'd been there!' groaned Carlotta. 'Go on. What happened?'

'Well, when the car saw the caravan by the light of its headlamps, it stopped, of course,' said Jim. 'We pretended that our caravan had got stuck, and we were pulling and heaving at it like anything. One of the men in the car jumped out to see what was up – and he called to the other man to come and help us so that we could shift the caravan out of his way. So I slipped off to the car, and there, in the back, all tied up like a chicken, with a handkerchief round her mouth, was your friend. I got her out in half a tick, of course, and bundled her behind a hedge.'

'Quick work!' said Carlotta, enjoying the tale thoroughly.

'Very quick,' agreed the man. 'Well, then I went back to the others, tipped them the wink, and we moved the caravan away in a jiffy, leaving the road clear. The two men went back to the car, hopped in, never looked behind at all to see if the girl was there – and drove off in the night without her!'

Carlotta began to laugh. It struck her as very funny indeed to think of the two kidnappers being so easily tricked and racing away in the night with an empty car!

'Whatever will they think when they take a look behind and see Sadie is gone?' she said. 'You did awfully well, Jim. Now we don't need to call in the police or have a fuss made or anything. I can just take Sadie back to the school and nobody needs to know anything about it. I'm sure Miss Theobald wouldn't want the papers to splash headlines all about the kidnapping of Miss Sadie Greene!'

'Come along and have a word with her,' said Jim. Carlotta went along with him, leading the horse by a lock of its thick mane. She came to a large caravan and went up the steps. Inside was Sadie, combing out her ruffled hair by the light of an oil-lamp. A woman was sitting watching her. Nobody appeared to think that anything extraordinary had happened. It seemed as if rescuing kidnapped girls was quite an ordinary thing to happen in the middle of the night! Not even Sadie was excited – but then, she seldom was!

'Hallo, Sadie,' said Carlotta. 'Doing Your Hair, as usual!'

'Carlotta!' said Sadie, in surprise. 'How did *you* get here? I was an awful idiot, I got kidnapped again. That note you opened by mistake was supposed to be from an old nanny of ours that I was very fond of – and I went out to see her – and two men caught me. And then somebody bundled me out and rescued me – but I haven't quite got the hang of things yet. And my hair got frightfully untidy, so I'm just putting it right.'

Carlotta grinned. 'If you fell out of an aeroplane you'd wonder if your hair was getting windblown!' she said. She told Sadie all that had happened, and how Prudence had followed her, thinking she was after Carlotta.

'Gracious!' said Sadie. 'What a night. I suppose we'd better go back to St Clare's, hadn't we?'

'Well, I think we had,' said Carlotta. 'You see, Sadie, I guess Miss Theobald won't want this story known all over the country – and I know the circus people won't want the police called in. They never do. So I think we'd better just go quietly back to school, and hush it all up. I've got a horse outside – a hunter I took from a field. Do you think you could manage to ride it with me?'

'I'm sure I couldn't,' said Sadie, promptly.

'Oh, well – you'll have to try, said Carlotta impatiently. 'You can put your arms round my waist and hang on to me. Come on!'

The two girls went to find the horse. Jim had it outside the caravan. Carlotta jumped up and spoke to Jim.

'Thanks for doing all you did,' she said. 'I won't forget it. Hold your tongue about everything, won't you?'

'You bet!' said Jim. 'It's all in a day's work. Come and see us again, Carlotta. I always say and I always shall say you're wasted at school – you ought to be in a circus like you've always been – handling horses. You're a marvel with them.'

'Ah well,' said Carlotta, 'things don't always happen as we want them to. Sadie, what are you doing? Surely you can jump up behind me?'

'I can't,' said Sadie. 'The horse seems so enormous.'

Jim gave her a heave and the surprised girl found herself sitting behind Carlotta. She clung to her with all her might. The horse set off at a gallop. Carlotta put him to jump the fence. Up he went with the two girls on his back and came down lightly the other side. Sadie squealed with fright. She had nearly fallen off.

'Let me off, oh, let me off!' she shouted. 'Carlotta, LET ME OFF!'

But Carlotta didn't. She galloped on through the starlit night, poor Sadie bumping up and down, up and down behind her.

'Oh,' gasped Sadie, 'tell the horse not to bump me so, Carlotta! Carlotta, do you hear?'

'It's you that are bumping the horse!' said Carlotta, with a squeal of laughter. 'Hang on, Sadie! Hang on!'

But it was too much for Sadie. When they had gone about half-way back, she suddenly loosened her hold on Carlotta, and slid right off the horse. She fell to the ground with a bump and gave a yell. Carlotta stopped the horse at once.

'Sadie! Are you hurt? Why did you do that?'

'I'm awfully bruised,' came Sadie's voice from the ground. 'Carlotta, I will NOT ride that bumpy horse another step. I'd rather walk.'

'How tiresome you are!' said Carlotta, springing lightly

to the ground. She pulled Sadie up and soon made sure that the girl was not really hurt. 'It will take us ages to get back. We shall have to walk all the way and I must lead the horse. We shan't get back till daylight!'

'I wonder what the others are thinking,' said Sadie, limping along beside Carlotta. 'I bet they're wondering and wondering what's happened!'

The others had worried and wondered till they were tired! They had all gone back to school, and had awakened the rest of the twins' dormitory. The girls had sat and discussed the night's happenings, wondering whether to go and tell Miss Theobald or not. Hilary at last decided that they really must. Carlotta and Sadie had not come-back, and Prudence was almost in hysterics. She really was frightened out of her life to think of the trouble that she had caused through being such a mischief-maker.

'Look – there's the dawn coming,' said Pat, looking to the east, where a pale silvery light was spreading. 'In another half-hour the sun will be up. For goodness' sake – let's tell Miss Theobald now. We can't wait for Carlotta any longer.'

So Pat and Isabel went down to awaken Miss Theobald, and the head listened in growing alarm to their curious tale. She had just reached out to take the telephone receiver in order to get in touch with the police when Pat gave a cry.

'Look! Look, Miss Theobald! There's Carlotta coming back – and she's got Sadie with her! Oh – good old Carlotta!'

Sure enough, there was Carlotta coming up the school grounds, with Sadie limping beside her. They had returned the hunter to its field and had come wearily up the school grounds just as the sun was rising. They had had a long way to walk and were very tired indeed.

Miss Theobald had them in her room in a trice, quite bewildered with the strange tale she had heard. She made the tired girls hot cocoa and gave them biscuits to eat. Then, to Carlotta's immense disgust, she took the sleepy girls across to the sickbay, woke up Matron, and bade her put the girls to bed in peace and quietness and keep them there.

'But Miss Theobald,' began Carlotta. Not a scrap of notice was taken of her, however, and it was not long before both she and Sadie were tucked up in comfortable beds and were sound asleep!

'If I had let them go back to their dormitory they would have talked until the dressing bell,' said Miss Theobald. 'Now go back to your beds too, you others, and we will sort things out in the morning. Really, I feel I must be dreaming all this!'

But it was no dream, and in the morning, as Miss Theobald had said, things had to be 'sorted out'.

It was decided that the matter must certainly be reported to the police, but kept as quiet as possible. Carlotta had the excitement of being interviewed by admiring policemen – and Prudence had the ordeal of being closely questioned too. She was frightened out of her life at it all. She had been able to lie and get away with so many unpleasant things before in her life – but there was no getting away with this.

'I want to go home,' she sobbed to Miss Theobald. 'I feel ill. Let me go home.'

'No,' said Miss Theobald. 'You want to run away from the troubles you have caused, Prudence. You are going to remain here and face them, however unpleasant things may be for you. Unless you want me to tell your parents everything, you will stay here and face things out. I hope this will be a lesson to you. I am not going to keep you at St Clare's after this term, of course. You will never be liked by any of the girls now. But you are going to learn a very bitter lesson for the rest of this term – and I hope, Prudence, you will derive some good from it. You need a punishment to make you learn what you have to learn.'

Sadie's mother had to be told about the attempted kidnapping and she arrived at St Clare's in a great state two weeks before the end of the term. She wanted to take Sadie away at once, but Miss Theobald persuaded her not to.

'You may be sure that such a thing will not be allowed to happen again now,' she said. 'If you wish, of course, you must take her away at the end of the term. Maybe you will want to take her back to America with you. Sadie is too grown up for St Clare's, Mrs Greene. If you *could* leave her for a term or two, so that she might shake down a little and try to become more of a schoolgirl, I should be delighted to have her. But maybe you don't want her to be an ordinary schoolgirl!'

Miss Theobald was right. Mrs Greene was like Alison, a feather-head! She had no brains at all, and her only interests in life were her clothes and entertaining others – and her precious pretty daughter, Sadie! She looked round at the girls of St Clare's, some with pig-tails, some with short hair, some freckled, some plain, some pretty.

'Well,' she said, 'don't you get sore at me for saying it, Miss Theobald – but I don't feel I want Sadie to be like these girls! My Sadie's pretty, and she's cute too. I wouldn't call any of these girls cute. Would you?'

'No, I wouldn't,' said Miss Theobald, smiling. 'We don't teach them to be "cute", Mrs Greene. We teach them to be independent, responsible, kind and intelligent, but we don't teach them to be "cute".'

'Well – I guess I'll leave Sadie here for the rest of the term, anyway,' said Mrs Greene, after a pause. 'I'll stay at the hotel down in the town and keep an eye on her. She seems fond of that pretty little thing called Alison. I'll let her stay on just for the rest of the term. Then I'll take her off to America again – and maybe Alison would like to come along too. She's about the cutest girl here.'

Miss Theobald made a private note in her mind to tell Alison's mother not to let her go with Sadie to America. She was not pleased with Alison that term. The girl had much better stuff in her than she had shown the last two or three months, and Miss Theobald did not want her to be completely spoilt.

So it came about that both Sadie and Prudence stayed on for the rest of the term and did not leave. Sadie was pleased – but Prudence was angry and unhappy. It was terribly difficult to face so many hostile girls every minute of the day. For the first time in her life she was really getting a punishment she deserved.

# 20

# The end of the term

And now the term drew swiftly to an end. There were tennis matches, swimming matches and other sports. There were, alas, exams too! The days were very full, and everyone had plenty to do from morning to night. The girls were very happy – all but Prudence, and nobody, not even Pam, felt sorry for the little humbug. No one knew she was leaving, and Prudence did not say a word about it.

Pam had been ill for a week or two – and Miss Theobald had come to the conclusion that her illness was due to over-work and unhappiness. Carlotta had told her about Pam's friendship with Prudence and how unhappy she had become about it.

'Now, Carlotta, you can do something for me,' said Miss Theobald. 'You can make friends with Pam, please, and see that Prudence does not try to get her under her thumb again. Pam is a good little thing, too advanced for her age – and it seems to me it will do her good to slack a little, instead of working so hard. Take her under your wing, Carlotta, and make her laugh a bit!'

Carlotta was surprised at this request, but rather proud. She had a great admiration for the sensible and wise head mistress, and the two understood each other very well. So, when Pam came out of the sickbay looking rather white and worn, and afraid that Prudence would attach herself to her once again, Pam had a pleasant surprise. Carlotta always seemed to be there! Carlotta pushed Prudence off, and asked Pam to go for walks with her instead, and got her to help her with her prep. Pam soon felt much happier, and her small face glowed whenever Carlotta came up.

'It's been a funny term, hasn't it?' said Miss Roberts to Mam'zelle. 'First of all I thought the new girls were never going to settle down and work – and I gave up Bobby in despair.'

'Ah, that Bobby!' said Mam'zelle, lifting her hands as she remembered all Bobby's tricks. 'That Bobby! But now she has turned over a new stalk – no, what is it you say – a new leaf – and she works and she works!'

'Yes – something has certainly happened to Bobby,' said Miss Roberts. 'She's using her brains – and she's got good ones too. I'm pleased with her. I'm going easy with little Pam Boardman though – she's inclined to work too hard.'

Mam'zelle smiled. 'Ah yes – but now that she has Carlotta for a friend, she does not work so hard. Always we have to hold Pam back or she would over-work herself – she does not play enough. But Carlotta will help her to do that. It is odd, that friendship.'

'I shouldn't be surprised if the head has something to do with it,' said Miss Roberts. 'She's a very remarkable woman, you know. She knows the girls inside-out.'

'Well – I hear that both Prudence and Sadie are leaving,'

said Mam'zelle. 'That is good. Ah, that Prrrrrrrudence! How I detest her!'

'She has a lot of lessons to learn in life,' said Miss Roberts, seriously. 'She has been taught a very big one here, and has learnt for the first time to see herself as she really is – and for two or three weeks she has to undergo the ordeal of knowing that others see her as she is, too. Ah, well – I don't know how she will turn out. She's a problem – and I'm glad I haven't got to solve it!'

'Sadie will not be missed either,' said Mam'zelle. 'Except by silly little Alison. She has had her head turned properly by that American girl. Ah, how cross they have both made me this term!'

Miss Roberts laughed. 'Yes – you've been in some fine tempers this term, Mam'zelle,' she said. 'But never mind – the term will soon be at an end – then summer holidays – and no tiresome girls to teach!'

'And when September comes, we shall both be saying, "Ah, how nice it will be to see those tiresome girls again!"' laughed Mam'zelle.

The girls were sorry that the summer term was coming to an end. Margery Fenworthy won the tennis championship for the school, and also the swimming matches. Carlotta won the diving. Bobby put up a record for the first form in swimming under water and was loudly cheered and clapped. Nobody was more surprised than she was!

'You deserve it, Bobby,' said Belinda, clapping her on the back. 'My word, how you've improved in tennis and

179

swimming. I'm proud of you, Don't-Care Bobby!'

Bobby felt happy. Her work had improved as much as her sports, and she had felt a new self-respect and contentment. Janet worked well too, now that Bobby was working, and the twins followed suit.

'You'll be able to go up into the second form next term, and do me credit,' said Miss Roberts, as she gave out the exam marks. 'Bobby, you are top in geography! Simply marvellous! Pam, you have done very well indeed. You O'Sullivan twins have managed to tie for second place in most things – that's very good. Hilary, you are top of the form, as you should be! Prudence, Doris, Alison and Sadie are, I regret to say, settling down near the bottom as usual. The great surprise is Carlotta, who has done far better than I expected! I think, Pam, that your help has done a good deal towards putting Carlotta into a higher place than I expected.'

Pam glowed with pleasure. Carlotta looked surprised and amused. Miss Roberts went on with her remarks, picking out each girl and commenting shrewdly on their term's work and exam results. Most of the first-form girls, with the exception of Pam, who was too young, were to go up into the second form the next term.

. 'That's good,' said Janet, afterwards. 'We shall all keep together now – and the two we like least, Sadie and Prudence, won't be here. I overheard by accident something Mam'zelle said in her loud voice to Miss Roberts. Well – I must say it's good news that Prudence won't be back.'

'Won't she really?' said Janet. 'Well, I vote if that's

so, we're a bit nicer to her then. She's looking pretty miserable lately.'

So for the last two or three days of term the girls relaxed their hostile attitude towards Prudence and the girl regained some of her confidence and happiness. She had begun to learn her lesson, though, and made no attempt to boast or to lie, as she always used to do. Poor Prudence – she was her own worst enemy, and always would be.

The last day came, and the usual wild rush of packing and saying goodbye. Margery Fenworthy proudly packed the beautiful racket she had won for her tennis prize. Bobby just as proudly packed her swimming-underwater prize – a lovely new swimming-costume. All the girls were happy and excited.

'It's a shame I can't come to America with you,' said Alison to Sadie, half-tearful at the thought of saying goodbye to her friend. 'I can't think why Mother won't let me. Don't forget me, Sadie, will you?'

'Of course not,' said Sadie, quite meaning what she said – but the girl was incapable of remembering anyone for long! Her real interest in life was herself and her looks – her friends would never last with her! But Alison did not know this and squeezed Sadie's arm tightly. She knew she would miss her terribly.

The last minutes came. Goodbyes were shouted as the school-coach came up to the door for the first batch of girls. Mam'zelle screamed as someone dropped a suitcase on her toes.

'Pat! *Que vous êtes . . .*' she began. And a whole chorus of girls finished her sentence for her . . .

'Abominable!' There was a shriek of laughter as they tried to get away from Mam'zelle's large hands, dealing out friendly slaps all the way round.

'Goodbye, Miss Roberts,' said the twins. 'Goodbye, Miss Roberts,' said Bobby. 'Goodbye, Miss Roberts,' said all the other first formers one by one.

'Goodbye, girls,' said Miss Roberts. 'Well – you won't stand in awe of me any more next term! You'll all be second formers, very important indeed – and I'll be left behind with the first form! Dear me – to think how you all grow up!'

'They'll long to be back with you, Miss Roberts!' laughed Miss Jenks, who was nearby. 'My goodness, they don't know what a dragon they are coming to, next term. How I'll make them work! What terrible punishments I shall have in store for them! How I shall see through all their tricks!'

The girls laughed. They liked Miss Jenks, and were looking forward to going up into her class. It would be fun. A new class and a new teacher – yes, they really would have fun!

The first formers got into the coach that was waiting for them. Alison heaved herself up, and her hat went crooked and then fell off. The girls stared at her hair.

'Alison! You've done your hair all funny again!' cried Pat. 'Piled it all on top as if you were twenty-one or something. You *do* look a freak! Honestly you do.'

Alison went red. She put her hat on again and turned defiantly to the twins.

'Well, Sadie says . . .' she began. And at once, in the greatest delight the whole coachful of girls took up the chorus they knew so well, and chanted it all the way down to the station.

'Sadie says – Sadie says – what does Sadie *say*? Sadie says – oh, Sadie says – what does Sadie *say*?'

And there we will leave them, first formers for the last time, singing on their way home for the holidays. What will happen to them when they are important second formers? Ah – that is another story altogether!

Don't miss the next exciting St Clare's story ...

*Enid Blyton*

## The Second Form at
# ST CLARE'S

The twins and their friends are planning a
concert and a very special midnight feast, but
will spiteful Elsie ruin it all?

**There's mischief at St Clare's!**